The Prairie Man

Tales about the spectre of the night known as the Prairie Man were told to frighten children, but one day those tales nearly led to a tragic accident for Temple Kennedy. His friend Hank Pierce saved his life, Temple vowed that one day he would return the favour.

Fifteen years later the two friends grew up to lead different lives: Hank is a respected citizen while Temple is an outlaw. But, when Hank is wrongly accused of murder, Temple is given a chance for redemption. He vows to save Hank or die in the attempt.

However, in seeking to unmask the real culprit his investigation leads to a man who isn't even supposed to exist: the Prairie Man.

The Prairie Man

I.J. Parnham

ROBERT HALE · LONDON

Typeset by
Derek Doyle & Associates, Shaw Heath
Printed and bound in Great Britain by
CPI Antony Rowe, Chippenham and Eastbourne

PROLOGUE

'The Prairie Man is coming!' Hank Pierce screeched. He grabbed Temple Kennedy's shoulder and tried to move him on along the top of the bank.

Temple dug in his heels while wondering how to glean some amusement out of the situation, but when he saw that Hank's shocked eyes were glistening with moisture in the moonlight he took pity on him.

'He isn't,' he said. 'The Prairie Man's not real. He's just a story your ma made up.'

Hank gulped, showing that he wanted to believe him, but that he was genuinely scared.

'But it wasn't like she said. This time he was real. We should never have sneaked out.'

Temple shook his head. The two years he had on the ten-year-old Hank had let him work out that they'd been told scary stories about a dark shadow that flitted through the darkness to stop them sneaking out late at night. That hadn't stopped them, but right now Hank clearly wished it had.

Beside them the narrow creek's water was an inky mass with the steep banks on either side keeping the low moonlight from penetrating. The shrouded banks held the promise of adventure, but their home was in the only direction that Hank wanted to go.

Temple gestured ahead. 'We'll go home, then. But be quiet or we'll be in deep trouble.'

'We are already. The Prairie Man is after us.'

Hank wailed, then hurried on. His voice sounded so worried that Temple looked back along the bank. Other than the tall grass that was waving in the light breeze he could see only the lone oak thirty yards away, its stark and gnarled form perhaps providing a clue about what Hank's active imagination had really seen.

Temple set off after him, but in his haste to catch up his bare foot slipped on a patch of mud and he fell at full length. Worse, he rolled to the side and tumbled over the edge of the bank. Then he bumped down the steep side, his vision filled with whirling stars until with a gasp he hit the cold water.

Silence and darkness hit him and he felt strangely serene. He flapped his arms and the motion moved him to the surface where he shook the water from his eyes and looked up the bank.

Hank had stopped and he was looking down at

him, making Temple's heart thud with embarrassment. Once Hank had calmed down he would have been able to rib him about how scared he had been, but after falling into the water Hank could easily rib him back about his foolishness.

Temple was a good swimmer, so he kicked off towards the side. He didn't move, so he tried again, but this only succeeded in dragging him backwards. He slipped under the water and he had to fight to get back to the surface, where he needed to crane his neck to keep his head above water.

'Help,' he gasped before he again went under.

This time he gathered his strength and kicked out, but that showed him what his problem was. Vegetation had snagged his right foot and the more he kicked, the more the weeds wound around his ankle. He again reached the surface, but Hank hadn't moved.

'Stop playing around and get out,' Hank urged in hushed tones.

'I'm trapped,' Temple shouted, uncaring of who heard him now. He waved his arms frantically, but still he couldn't move forward. 'Something's caught me.'

'The Prairie Man?'

'Weeds,' Temple managed to gasp before he went under.

He hadn't gathered a strong breath and the urge to open his mouth for air tore at his lungs, but he

7

fought back the panic that made his guts churn. He ran his hands down to his legs. He felt the loops of weed that infested this slow-moving part of the creek and he yanked them away, but there were so many and he felt so tired.

A hand touched soft silt, then his side rested on the bottom. The feeling wasn't as worrying as he'd expected. He could curl up here and sleep just as comfortably as back in his bed. He opened his mouth and yawned.

He gasped in a huge gulp of air.

He coughed and spluttered, then gasped again and retched. That made him feel better and when he looked up he found that he was no longer in the water. Hank had put aside his fears and had dragged him out of the creek.

'You'll be fine, won't you?' Hank asked, concern for him having driven away his childish fears about a spectre in the night.

'I will be, thanks to you.' Temple sat up. 'Let's go home.'

Later that night, wrapped up in a blanket with their warming bodies pressed up close and with their wet clothes drying on the windowsill, the two excitable boys found sleep hard to come by.

'Temple,' Hank whispered, 'tell me the truth. You don't believe I saw the Prairie Man, do you?'

'I don't.'

'But I saw a shadow gliding along on the other

8

side of the creek. I did, I really did.' He gulped. 'That makes me a child, doesn't it?'

Sometimes it was all right to poke fun at his younger friend, but Temple had heard the fear in his voice.

'No. What you did tonight makes you a man. You saved my life. If it hadn't have been for your bravery, I'd be dead, just like my parents.'

Temple's parents had died last month and Hank's family had taken him in, but Temple hadn't spoken about this matter before with Hank or with anyone else. Silence somehow kept alive the hope he'd been told a lie and they'd come back for him.

'I wouldn't want that.'

Temple detected the stronger tone of his friend's voice. Even if they weren't brothers by blood, they were treated like brothers now, and that thought made Temple feel determined that something should change tonight.

They had acted like silly children, but they had also been through something that was very adult. It was a secret thing they could never tell Hank's parents and especially not Hank's talkative younger sister Kate.

Temple picked up the oil lamp beside the bed. Beneath was the knife he was allowed to whittle with but which Hank wasn't allowed to touch yet, even if he had done so from the first day he'd moved here.

Temple took the knife, then sat up in bed. Hank

shuffled round to watch him.

Temple raised a thumb, steeled himself, then pricked it. He bit his lip to avoid squealing, then passed the knife to Hank who, without being asked, did the same.

While Hank gulped to avoid showing it'd hurt, Temple took his hand, then held the thumb up to the light beside his, showing the bright bubbles of blood. He pressed the two thumbs together and although the cut made him wince it felt the right thing to do.

'Now we're brothers in blood too,' he said.

'We are,' Hank said happily.

Temple felt he should say something more, so when Hank moved to suck his thumb he held it firmly.

'Tonight you saved my life, so one day I must save yours. When we grow up we might travel far away from here, but no matter where we go, you will always know that however much trouble you are in, I owe my life to you.'

Hank rubbed his nose with the back of his hand while fighting back the tears that had never been far away tonight.

'You won't go away, will you?'

Temple looked through the window at the grass undulating in the moonlight. The urge to explore that had dominated his thoughts since last month's events and which had led to tonight's adventure overcame him again, but he shrugged.

'I don't know, but I do know that no matter where I go, if you ever need me, I will find you and I will save you.'

CHAPTER 1

'How much longer will they be?' Temple Kennedy said while peering down the trail towards Bear Creek.

'Patience,' Cad Miller said. 'They're probably being careful.'

Temple laughed, acknowledging that Luther Duval and Burton Sibley were the kind of men who were good at riding into town a-shooting and a-hollering, but not sneaking in and out of town quietly.

'You reckon this'll end in trouble?'

Cad cast him an odd look. 'Why else do you think they promised us both fifty dollars if we waited here?'

Temple shrugged. 'I don't know. I needed the money, so I didn't ask too many questions.'

'I needed the money too, but I still asked. Luther heard a rumour that a mercantile owner Bill Ellis hides his money in a hole at the back of his store.

Burton's been working for him and he now knows where it is. They're digging it up tonight.'

Temple gulped. 'You mean they're stealing it?'

The question made Cad open his eyes wide in surprise and, with a lurching feeling in his guts, Temple accepted he'd been stupid. He should have asked questions, no matter how much he'd needed the money and, either way, he should have worked out that they would be committing a crime. Why else would he and Cad be waiting fifteen miles out of town with fresh horses?

As it turned out, when he first caught sight of them they were riding fast with nobody in pursuit. But when they came closer Temple saw the sour expressions that said something had gone wrong, even if a bulging corn sack lay over Luther's saddle.

'Give me the reins,' Luther muttered the moment he'd drawn up. 'We haven't got time to waste.'

'Someone after you?' Cad asked.

'There will be,' Luther said with a glance at Burton that said they had a story to relate, even if they weren't prepared to tell it just yet.

Temple and Cad didn't ask what the problem was; and instead they mounted up. In short order they shooed away the tired horses. Then they turned away from the westward route the two men had been taking and headed north.

At high points they looked back, but they saw no sign of pursuit. Darkness came and still they rode on.

It was long into the night when they fetched up in the one-road town of Big Springs. There was nowhere to sleep here other than the stables, but apparently Luther and Burton had stopped here before.

Big Springs was a settlement that asked no questions and more important, it would provide no answers to anyone who might later ask where they'd gone.

They would have to leave before first light, and split up to confuse any pursuers, but tonight they had enough time to relax their frazzled nerves with a few whiskeys. Cad smiled when he saw that the sack contained several hundred dollars, but Luther and Burton maintained their sour moods.

Temple waited until they'd each knocked back two large whiskeys before he broached the subject of what was troubling them.

'What happened back there?' he asked.

They were sitting in a quiet corner of a quiet saloon where nobody was interested in anyone else's business, but even so Luther looked around to check nobody was near before he replied.

'It went wrong,' he said, drawing the men into a conspiratorial huddle. 'We dug the hole quietly, but not quietly enough. While Burton was keeping watch Bill found me.'

Temple and Cad exchanged worried glances before they leaned forward again to hear the rest.

14

'How badly hurt?' Cad asked.

'It wasn't Bill,' Luther said. He glanced at Burton, who frowned.

'I broke a plank over Bill's head,' Burton said. 'He went down, but he was breathing all right, so I headed round to the front with the sack. Luther didn't follow.'

'This young lad had found us,' Luther added with a pronounced gulp.

'His nephew stays with him sometimes,' Burton said with another gulp. 'But not any more.'

'You couldn't have killed him,' Temple muttered.

'I didn't intend to,' Luther said. He knocked back a whiskey and poured another. 'He shouted for help, so I put a hand over his mouth, then carried him to the storeroom. I meant to gag him, but I took a while to find a rag. When I took the hand away. . . .'

Luther looked around at the men with his upper lip curled in horror.

'He was a weak lad and he had trouble breathing,' Burton said. 'The shock would have been too great for him.'

Nobody said that this fact meant Luther shouldn't blame himself. He *was* to blame for this. They all were.

For several minutes the four men sat without saying a word, but when Cad broke the stillness by moving to refill everyone's glasses, Temple shook his head and stood.

'Not for me,' he said.

'Where you going?' Cad asked.

'The whiskey don't taste too good no more. I'm getting some fresh air.'

With that, Temple turned on his heels, walked out of the saloon, and headed to the stables.

Five minutes later he was riding out of town. He didn't have a destination in mind, but he was several miles out of Big Springs before he realized that Luther had slipped his payment into his pocket.

He had to stop to vomit.

Three days after the disastrous robbery Temple was holed up in another dead-end town. It was so neglected it didn't appear to have a name and he didn't feel inclined to talk to anyone to find out if it did in fact have one.

He still had all the money he'd been paid and the sight of it made him feel like the lowest snake in the world. He had led a drifting life that had avoided responsibility, but he had never been involved in a criminal act before and he didn't like the man he now felt he'd become.

He was tempted to throw the money away, but somehow that felt too easy. He had to spend every dollar he'd helped to steal and feel the shame every time. So he embarked on a mission to drink his money away.

He devoted two days to steadily consuming liquor,

but he still failed to spend all his funds. Then a fight over something he'd been too drunk to remember resulted in him being thrown out of town. So he moved on and sought other ways to lose the rest of his money.

The next town was Redemption City, an imposing settlement with saloons catering for the lowest as well as the best. Temple had had enough of slinking around with his fellow dregs, and so he headed to a lively gambling-house.

He got into a poker-game with the most purposeful looking players he could find, then proceeded to see how fast he could lose the last of his money.

He failed at that too.

His betting without care or logic worried the other players into believing he was using a clever system, so quickly did he accumulate funds. So he bet heavily on a hand where he didn't even look at his hole and river cards.

Nobody spotted his reckless behaviour, so he was able to lock horns with a sweating businessman who was trying to give the impression he had a full house.

The confrontation drew a small crowd, who murmured their delight when at the showdown it turned out that the businessman had a full house, after all. The trouble was, when Temple turned over his cards he found he'd been dealt two kings giving him four of a kind.

He'd never had that kind of luck before, but he

knew when he was beaten, so he stood up from the table. The businessman accepted his play with good grace and Temple walked out of the saloon with $500 in his pocket. He walked away slowly, but nobody followed him out to steal the money.

At a loss to figure out how he could get rid of money he didn't want, he stopped outside a mercantile. He admired a shiny saddle and a new set of clothes, but that got him thinking that there was one hard-working man who wouldn't be enjoying selling such items any more.

Feeling wretched again he resumed walking. When he reached a hotel he decided he would sleep in a decent bed tonight. In the morning, after a full night's sleep, he might be able to decide what he should do next. But the hotel turned out to be fully booked and the owner turned him away.

When he was back out on the boardwalk two smartly dressed men went in, giving him a wide berth. Temple watched them through the doorway and he saw that they had no trouble getting rooms.

Temple looked down at himself. His clothes were torn and stained, and when he rubbed his chin he found a straggly beard.

Somehow more time had passed than he'd thought. But his ragged clothing shouldn't have been enough to make the hotel owner look at him with so much contempt that he wouldn't let him sleep in a decent hotel. He stood before the hotel window and sought an angle that let him see his reflection.

The light was bright enough to expose his face, but he couldn't see the eyes. They were deep-set and even without seeing them he knew they were haunted.

He looked like a desperate man, a man people avoided.

'What's happened to me?' he asked. His statement made two passing men look at him oddly, so he moved away across the road.

A church was on the opposite side. He hadn't been in one since he'd left his childhood home ten years ago, but he felt an urge to do so now. The church door was locked.

He did, though, find a banner plastered to a notice board. It said: *Seek the Redemption Trail and Ye Shall be Saved.*

Temple smiled.

CHAPTER 2

'Don't you remember me?' Temple asked.

'I don't,' Philip Stiles said with a weary air. 'How much do I owe you?'

'Nothing. I owe you.'

Philip peered at him. 'Don't reckon so. I never forget a face that I need to, and I've not met you before.'

'It was eight years ago.'

Philip waved a dismissive hand at him. 'Even I don't hold on to a debt for that long. Buy whatever you want now with hard cash and that'll be fine with me.'

Temple sighed, lost for the words that would explain himself.

Having decided to ride his personal redemption trail, he had faced a problem. He had wronged so many people with his drifting life and his failure to take responsibility for his actions that he was unsure where he should start.

He figured that he hadn't been directly involved in the incident in which Luther had killed the kid, so he should start at the beginning, when it had all started going wrong.

Philip Stiles was that beginning.

After leaving his home in Prudence by riding the rails for as long as he could cope with the cold wind and the hunger he'd ended up here. Philip had been good to him, giving him work.

For two years he'd worked hard and been a good employee. But eventually he had been worn down by a lack of a direction in life, combined with the envy he felt whenever he served the seemingly endless stream of customers who were richer than he was.

There had to be something better than this and he had convinced himself that it lay in Monotony, the big town to which the stage that stopped outside the mercantile headed.

A ticket cost five dollars and he'd saved to buy one, except someone found his money and stole it. He didn't want to start putting aside nickels and dimes again, so he worked out how much he reckoned Philip had underpaid him over the years, decided that it was five dollars, then took the money from the till. Then he bought a ticket and started his drifting life.

He doubted Philip wanted to hear all this, so he kept to the basics.

'I don't want to buy anything. I was just passing through, but I figure I wronged you. I used to work for you and I took . . .' He sighed. 'I stole, I guess, five dollars. I want to return it.'

Philip pushed back his hat in puzzlement, but then his eyes narrowed as he placed him.

'Temple Kennedy?'

'Sure.' Temple withdrew five dollar bills from his pocket and put them on the counter.

Philip cast the money a disdainful glare. 'You were idle and a dreamer. I rejoiced when you left, figuring five dollars was a fair price if I never had to clap eyes on your worthless hide again. And I don't want to see you or your money now.'

Philip turned his back on him and busied himself behind the counter. Temple could do nothing but take his unwanted money and leave.

If he were to follow his trail of mistakes in an attempt to put them right, his next stop would be Monotony. He figured he'd have better luck there. He was wrong.

He couldn't find the ostler who had lost his job when ten horses had been stolen while Temple should have been looking after the stables, but instead had been sleeping off the effects of his first trip to a saloon.

In Carmon, the sheep farmer who had lost twenty animals when they'd wandered off into the river while he'd been dallying with the farmer's daughter in the barn remembered him. As did the daughter and the husband she'd not told him about. They chased him away and he didn't get the chance to apologize.

The highlight of his mission to live a better life by righting his past failings came in Beaver Ridge. Two years ago he'd worked as a bartender, but one night he'd sampled too many of the saloon's wares and he had fallen over while sweeping up. He'd accidentally knocked over an oil lamp and the saloon had burnt down.

The owner was delighted to see him.

It turned out that he had hated his saloon and the loss of the building had made him change his priorities. He'd rebuilt the saloon twice as big as before. He'd made a fortune. The owner treated him to a drink and even introduced him to his customers as being the man who had changed his life.

Two months after embarking on his redemption trail Temple was no longer sure what he had hoped to achieve and he had spent most of his ill-gotten money trying to find people who might want it. But for his last visit, money wasn't required.

A month before Luther had recruited him and then, later, Cad in a saloon in Bear Creek he'd come close to making the best decision of his life, except he'd not had the courage to see it through.

The first hints that this time also it wouldn't go well came when he rode through the ranch gates.

'You're too late, Temple,' a ranch hand called.

Temple didn't know the man's name, but then again he hadn't paid much attention to the running of the ranch.

Someone must have called ahead as the one person he had paid attention to emerged from around the back of the ranch house. She was wringing water from her hands with the air of someone who had been busy, but when she saw who was approaching she stopped and considered him with her hands on her hips.

'Lucille,' he said, drawing his horse to a halt.

'You're too late,' she said.

'What does that mean?'

'It means I got married last week.'

Temple winced, proving to himself that he had hoped he'd get something more than just redemption from this particular encounter. He masked his disappointment by dismounting.

'I'm pleased for you. Who out of all your admirers won your heart?'

'You don't know him. Mark was a ranch hand who arrived looking for work after you'd left.'

Lucille cocked her head to one side, letting him fill in the details for himself. It was likely that this relationship had followed the same path as theirs had, and it had finished with the result that Temple had run to avoid.

'He's a lucky man.'

An awkward silence ensued allowing time for a thickset man to emerge from the house, cast them a suspicious look, then move towards them. Temple presumed he was Mark and his arrival flustered Lucille.

'Now that you know I won't be taking you back,' she said, speaking quickly before Mark joined them, 'you can go.'

'That's not why I'm here. I came to apologize. I treated you badly and I reckon you deserve an explanation.'

Lucille narrowed her eyes, her brow furrowing, but with her being lost for words, Mark had enough time to join them.

'What do you want?' he asked, standing ahead of her in a defensive position.

'Nothing,' Lucille said. 'He's leaving.'

Her voice caught, making Mark cast Temple an angry glare before he turned to her.

'Who is he?'

His authoritative voice made her frown. 'He's Temple Kennedy, the man who—'

She didn't get to complete her explanation before Mark swirled round to confront Temple.

'So you're the man who took advantage of my wife.'

'I reckon the only one who got taken advantage of was me.' Temple laughed. 'I wasn't the first, but it looks like you might be the last.'

As Lucille lowered her head to hide her shame-faced expression, Mark grunted with anger, then advanced a long pace towards Temple. He threw back his fist and launched a scything blow at his face. Temple thrust up an arm to protect himself, but the punch brushed it aside and caught him a glancing blow to the cheek that sent him to one knee.

Quickly he jumped to his feet, then moved backwards to avoid a fight he didn't want, but Mark had other ideas. He hurried on and with a roll of the shoulders he caught Temple with a running blow to the chin that toppled him like a felled tree.

'Stop that, Mark,' Lucille cried. 'He doesn't mean any harm.'

Mark had gone beyond listening to reason. He bent down and took hold of Temple's vest front, then dragged him to his feet.

Temple stood stooped and swaying, his senses reeling, and so was unable to defend himself when Mark pummelled his right cheek so strongly that he went staggering away for several paces until he fell to his knees.

'Get up, you good-for-nothing piece of trash,' Mark demanded standing over him.

Temple stared down at the ground, gathering his strength with deep breaths. A part of him felt strangely pleased that at last someone was making him pay for his failings, but anger was also dulling his mind.

He waited until Mark moved to drag him upright again. Then he kicked off from the ground and with a leading shoulder he slammed into Mark's guts and carried him backwards for several paces until Mark slipped. Mark sprawled forward over Temple's back. Bent double, Temple was able to brace himself, then toss Mark backwards for him to land on his back in a cloud of dust.

Temple felt his bruised cheek as he paced round to stand over Mark. He was ready to turn the tables and inflict a beating of his own, but Lucille placed a hand on his shoulder.

'If you came to apologize,' she said, 'don't do this.'

His anger leaked away and he moved back, letting her go to Mark, who was limiting himself to glaring up at him.

When he got to his feet Temple saw that Mark had landed awkwardly and that he was rubbing his hip. Lucille wrapped an arm around his shoulders and, with a hobbling gait that slowly became more assured he let her lead him to the ranch house.

When the door closed behind them Temple turned on the spot. Several ranch hands were watching him from a distance while fingering farm implements with obvious intent, but he still headed to a water trough.

He splashed water on his face, finding that the fight had given him a split lip, which he dabbed at until the bleeding stopped. Then he moved to his horse, but to his surprise Lucille had returned.

'I did come here to apologize,' he said, 'and not to fight. I'm sorry I ran. I had a bad start as a kid and that turned me into a drifter who never knows what's good for him. I've always hoped I'd find something better beyond the horizon, except when I found it here with you that scared me. I hope you're happy with Mark. He seems like a good man who'll protect you.'

'He is,' Lucille said. 'He's certainly more of a man than you are. You leaving was the best thing that could have happened to me.'

Temple fingered his cut lip while he fought the urge to admit that she wasn't the first to say this.

'I'm sorry. That's all I wanted to say.' He tipped his hat and moved to go by her.

'That was harsh of me,' she said, softening her tone. She stepped to the side to stop him leaving, then glanced around, clearly wanting to say something more, but finding it hard to speak. Then she brightened and withdrew a letter from behind her back. 'You need to read this.'

'If that's how you prefer to talk to me, I understand.'

'The letter's not from me. It arrived two weeks ago. It'd been around a few places, but it ended up here and I didn't know where you'd gone. I read it and I'm sorry: the news is bad.'

Temple took the letter and considered it, then smiled.

'Goodbye, Lucille. Have a good life.'

'If you'd. . . .' She took a pace closer, a hand reaching out to grip his arm. 'If you'd come even a day before Mark and I wed. . . .'

Then, as if she'd said enough already, she left the thought uncompleted and lowered her hand. She hurried back to the house.

Temple watched her go, the revelation she had almost made giving him some comfort that perhaps he had learnt something valuable here that would help him to move on. With his head held high, he rode away from the ranch. He even called out to several ranch hands.

A few miles on he stopped beside the river where he and Lucille had often picnicked. He read the letter. It was from Hank Pierce, his foster-brother, a man he hadn't seen for ten years. And as promised, it was bad news.

It also gave him everything he'd been searching for.

CHAPTER 3

The town of Prudence had grown in the ten years since Temple had left.

The railroad track that had taken him away had just arrived back then. Now it had brought prosperity, transforming a humble collection of homesteads into a thriving and bustling town. Even in the heat of the early afternoon more people were about than had once lived in the whole settlement.

The reek of sizzling steaks and pungent perfume assailed him. On either side of the heavily rutted roads people crowded the boardwalks. With new buildings spreading down one side of the railroad Temple even found it hard to orient himself.

He had to find the creek to get his bearings. Even then he made the mistake of heading in the wrong direction before he doubled back and made his way to the row of homesteads where Hank's parents had lived. But this area had changed too.

The dugouts and sod-houses were derelict. Only one building was in a maintained state, but this was a log construction. Only when Temple found that the old oak was still hanging on to life on the top of the bank did he work out that this house was on the site of the old house where he'd lived.

Nobody was in and the building had the cold feeling of having been abandoned for a while. He investigated and fifty yards away, at a point that let him look down on the creek and to the town five miles away, he found two grave mounds.

They were overgrown, but fresh cut flowers lay here, and there were small stones on which were etched the names of Hank's parents, or as he realized with a shock, his own in some way. They had been good people who had cared for him for several years. The mistakes he'd made in life had been his own and not their fault.

Thoughtfully he rearranged the flowers. Then he returned to the creek, picking out the spot where his life could have ended if Hank hadn't dragged him out of the water. With that memory giving him renewed purpose he headed back to town.

In the first saloon on the road he asked about Hank. With so many new people being around nobody recognized him, but even so he gathered several harsh looks and refusals to answer before he got the information he wanted. It wasn't the news he had feared the most, but it was bad enough.

He headed to the law office on the edge of town. The long building incorporated a jailhouse and a courtroom. On duty was the first man to recognize him, Morgan Simmons, although he was now Sheriff Simmons.

'Temple Kennedy,' Simmons said, considering him with a lively gleam in his eyes. 'I never expected to see you again.'

'And I never expected to see you being a lawman.'

'I'm surprised. After all the times I had to chase you off my land when you and Hank were up to mischief, you ought to have remembered I was keen on justice.'

'I did, and I suppose I ought to thank you. The beatings taught me plenty.' Temple winked. 'They taught me to run faster.'

Simmons snorted a laugh, but then he cast him a sober look, acknowledging the reason why he'd come.

'Hank is my only guest. You can have fifteen minutes with him.'

'Obliged,' Temple said, then raised his arms as Simmons searched him. He didn't pack a gun, but Simmons was thorough, confirming that the situation was as bad as he'd been led to believe.

He was escorted through an iron-studded door with a barred window into the stone-built annexe in which there were four cells with each one standing apart from the one beside it. As promised the last

32

cell was the only occupied one.

When Simmons had left him Temple paced along, his footfalls clopping on the stone floor, but the prisoner Hank didn't look up from where he was lying back on his cot. Temple sat on a bench in the corner. Lost for the right thing to say he waited for Hank to speak first.

A minute passed until, with a long sigh, Hank rolled over.

'Did he let you bring in your pie this time, Kate?' he asked.

Temple noted that this comment meant that his foster-sister was still in town; a meeting with her was sure to be more comfortable than this one was. Hank's voice was unrecognizable from the one he'd last heard when, late one night, he'd told him of his plans to leave. He was also thin and smaller than Temple would have expected the boy who had been taller than him to become.

'No pie,' Temple said.

'Then go away, whoever you are. I'm busy.'

Temple laughed. 'You don't look busy.'

This had been Hank's father's traditional comment whenever they'd tried to get out of doing a task. Hank must have picked up on it as he shot up to a sitting position on his cot and considered him.

'Temple, is that really you?'

'I got your letter. It took a while to find me.'

Hank moved to get off the cot, but then he

flopped back down on it, as if he were ashamed to come too close. He leaned back against the bars.

'I always hoped you'd come back one day, but I didn't want to get my wish granted like this.'

'I wish there was some other way too.' Temple frowned. 'What happened?'

'When I grew up I turned into a vicious murderer.'

'I know,' Temple said, using a deadpan tone. 'I've been told about your terrible life of crime, but what made you turn out so bad?'

Hank mustered a thin smile. 'It's good to hear you again, it really is. They say I killed James Merritt, and just about the only person who believes I didn't do it is Kate.'

James had been one of the original settlers. Temple couldn't remember much about him or his brother Emerson other than that they lived on the north side of the creek and that they were as good at chasing him and Hank away as Morgan Simmons had been.

'And me now.' Temple waited until Hank nodded. 'What makes the others think you did it?'

Hank sighed. 'Since you left, life here has been good. Few of the people who were here before are still around, but the railroad's brought plenty of newcomers and they're prospering, as was I.'

'I've only just arrived, but I've seen enough to work that out.'

'What you wouldn't have seen is that James wanted to expand his territory to the south of the creek. He started buying out the original settlers. I hung on the longest, but in the end I had to accept that I could just sell up and move. I went to sign his papers, but instead I found his dead body. He'd been shot.'

'From what I remember he was a decent man, tough but fair. He didn't deserve that.'

'He didn't, so the sight shocked me. I turned his body over and got blood all over my hands.' Hank raised his hands to look at them, turning them over then back again as if the blood was still there. 'Then I went to the door, but Sheriff Simmons had arrived. It looked bad. I don't blame him for reaching the wrong conclusion.'

'A jury is sure to look at it differently.'

'They didn't. They took an hour to find me guilty.'

Temple winced. 'And what are you waiting for now?'

'I'm waiting to die. I have two days. Then they hang me.'

Temple stood from the bench so quickly he toppled it. He went to the cell. Now knowing that the situation was even more urgent than he'd feared, the words he'd rehearsed came tumbling out, but they sounded more garbled than when he'd thought them through beforehand.

'When we were kids you saved my life.' He raised

a thumb, indicating the place where once he'd nicked his flesh. 'I promised then that if you were ever in danger, I'd do anything to save you. I was late getting here, but I'm not too late. I will save you. I will.'

'Thank you,' Hank said.

There was nothing else either man could say to the other. Temple turned on his heels and strode purposefully to the door. And he kept moving purposefully until he arrived at James Merritt's house, five miles to the north of the creek.

Despite his promise, he had no idea how he could fulfil it, but starting by seeing the scene of the alleged murder felt like the right place to begin. He looked over the imposing ranch house, noting it presented an air of being abandoned, as Hank's house had.

The possibility of finding anything of interest seemed unlikely, but for the first time in weeks he was content. He had been searching for a way to right his past mistakes and now he had found someone who needed his help. Best of all, he wanted to help him, and not just because he had been riding his redemption trail.

He paced around the house, looking in windows. Then, with a guilty glance around, he noticed a metal tine. He used it to prise open a door at the back.

He soon found the room in which James had

died. It provided him with no obvious clues as to what had happened other than to let him picture the scene that would have confronted Hank.

Set before a full-length broken mirror he found a dark patch on the floor that could have been blood. He moved back to the door, imagining walking in and finding the body. From here he could see through windows that looked out to the front and the back, making it hard for a killer to have sneaked away unseen. So whoever did it must have been gone for some time.

Temple shrugged, unsure whether this information helped him, although information was what he needed. The town had changed, so he didn't know most of the people. If he were to uncover the truth, he would need to understand what had been happening while he had been away.

In a thoughtful frame of mind he walked back to the door. It had swung fully open and now he looked it over, wondering how he could wedge it back into position to mask that he'd broken in.

A solid shove to his back knocked him to his knees.

He just had enough time to realize that someone had jumped him from behind when a second man stepped out of the shadows inside and aimed a sweeping kick at his jaw.

Temple jerked back and the boot parted air before his face, unbalancing the attacker. Temple put him from his mind and drove off from the floor while twisting.

He hit the man behind him solidly in the stomach with a rising shoulder and tipped him over. The man slammed into the wall, then went sprawling on to his back with a thud. Better still, he then rolled into the other man's legs and made him slip.

While both his assailants wasted valuable seconds righting themselves, Temple turned away. The open door was ahead, so, despite the intriguing possibility that this attack might be connected with earlier events here, he chose discretion. He ran out through the door, and walked into a second ambush.

Two men were on either side of the door, guns drawn and aimed at him.

'Reach,' one man said, 'and you'll live to explain yourself.'

'Relax,' Temple said, following the order. 'I'm not packing a gun.'

'We'll check that out before anyone relaxes.'

'Who are you?' Temple asked as one man moved in to frisk him.

'That question means you must be new around here. We're the Rangers, and you'd be well served to remember us.'

Temple noticed that both men wore matching blue jackets with a star-shaped emblem above the breast. When the other two men came outside he saw that they were clad in blue too.

'I'll remember. Now can I go?'

The men exchanged glances. Their small facial movements suggested that they were unsure how to answer. Temple, having got over the shock of being ambushed, noticed that they were all young and perhaps a little scared.

'We take him to George,' one man said.

'You mean Major Fowles,' another man said. 'That's his title and don't you forget it.'

Everyone winced, confirming that they'd erred and that they weren't as assured as they were trying to appear. But the declaration decided their course of action.

Temple promised to give them no trouble, figuring this encounter was at least introducing him to some interesting and unexpected aspects of life in Prudence. They rode back to the gates, then to the creek. They forded it and two miles along they reached an imposing house.

It was a two-storey wooden construction that was so impressive Temple wouldn't have expected to find such a home here even after seeing how prosperous Prudence had become.

They dismounted in front of the porch. Three men surrounded him while the other man headed inside. A few minutes later he emerged with another man, presumably Major George Fowles, who was shrugging into a blue jacket. He was about Temple's age and he projected authority as he marched towards him with a stiff back and his head held high.

'You've done well, Ranger Harris,' he said, addressing the man who had suggested coming here and making him shuffle from foot to foot with relief. 'These days the riches Prudence is accumulating attracts too many sharpers and we must always be on guard to repel them, no matter who their victims are.'

This speech made the men nod with delight and murmur congratulations to each other. Temple waited for silence.

'I'm no sharper,' he said.

George turned his attention on to Temple. He looked him up and down, then shrugged.

'Can you prove that?'

Temple held his hands wide apart. 'Search me. I have nothing stolen on me.'

'That's because you were caught before you could steal. Sheriff Simmons would have waited for you to commit your crime, then dealt with you, but we operate a more direct and more effective method. You will need better proof than that to convince me of your innocence.'

'And I can provide it,' a woman said from the doorway behind him.

George moved aside to let Temple see the new-comer walk across the porch. She sported a heavy bump that said a child was due and her fine features and mane of black hair tugged at his memory.

'Stay back, Kate,' George said, raising a hand. 'This man is trouble.'

'No, he isn't,' she said. 'He's Temple Kennedy, my foster-brother.'

CHAPTER 4

'I wish you could have returned in more pleasant circumstances,' Kate said.

Temple nodded. 'So do I.'

They had gone inside and they were now sitting in an ornate drawing room. So far George had stood back, considering him with a sceptical eye while the men who had brought him in looked on nervously, expecting reprisals. But since Kate and Temple were talking in pleasant tones, George appeared to accept that he was harmless. With a slap of a fist against his thigh he did a smart turn to face the other men.

'You men still did well,' he announced. 'You were vigilant and dealt with a potential threat.'

The men breathed sighs of relief before they cast apologetic glances at Temple. George then escorted them out while giving them orders to resume their patrol.

'Please forgive my husband,' Kate said with an

indulgent smile when they'd been left alone. 'He means well and he does keep them in line.'

'Who are these Rangers?'

'It was George's idea to protect the townsfolk. These last few years the town has grown and not everyone who has come has meant well. Everyone was getting worried and Sheriff Simmons . . . he's a good man and popular, but he was struggling to cope. But now we all feel safer.'

'I'm pleased you're safe, and I'm pleased you've found a good man.'

She nodded, then lowered her head to consider her hands. With a visible effort she released the tight grip she had of her skirt.

'I have. And what about you? You've grown into the fine-looking man I knew you would. What kind of life do you have?'

Temple looked around the room to avoid her noticing the guilty expression he was sure he must show whenever anyone mentioned his past activities.

'It's a drifting life. You know I liked the thought of always moving on.' He considered her rounded belly. 'But perhaps that life doesn't feel so appealing now that I've seen how content you are.'

She bit her lip, then manoeuvred herself to her feet to look through the window.

'I used to be content, but even with a family on the way I'm not happy and I doubt I ever will be if this ends badly.'

'I've already seen him,' Temple said, joining her. He placed a hand on her shoulder and gripped it. 'I made him a promise and I'll make you the same one. I will save him.'

'Do you really think you can prove he's innocent?' she said, swirling round to face him.

'No,' he said. He waited until her eyes opened wide with surprise before continuing. 'In this situation it's probably impossible to prove his innocence, so I'll do the one thing I can do: I'll find the man who really killed James Merritt.'

She nodded. 'I hope you can, as nothing I've tried has worked. George hired a good lawyer, but he couldn't help.'

'Was the evidence that strong?'

'I didn't think so, but then again I know Hank. Being found with blood on his hands after being seen arguing with James was strong enough to convince everyone.'

Temple hadn't known about the argument, but then he'd heard about the events only from Hank's viewpoint, so he pressed Kate to tell him everything, which she did at length. Then they turned to practical matters, and her posture relaxed. She painted a picture of a town going through change, but it didn't give Temple any ideas about where he could start.

The people Kate knew were decent citizens and she thought the best of them. Either someone wasn't who he seemed to be or Temple would have to become familiar with the kind of people Kate wouldn't know.

This last thought cheered him and it gave him an idea on where he'd start.

'That helped a lot,' he said when she'd finished. He offered her a wide grin.

She mustered a tentative smile. 'Perhaps I'll think of more details before we sit down to eat tonight.'

'I'm sorry, but I can't be there. I have people to see.' He noted her worried look. 'If I'm to work this out, I have to spend time in town, but I promise I'll eat with you soon, and we'll all be together.'

This last comment made her nod and after promising to keep her updated on his progress he left. He didn't see George or his men again as he headed into town to start on a task that his past life had helped him to perfect.

He ate in the most crowded eatery he could find, where he sat with two cowboys and encouraged their tales of their last drive and their impressions of the town. Then he toured the saloons, drinking little, but appearing to consume more. In each one he was boisterous and eager to join in whatever revelry was going on.

He reckoned the best way to not draw suspicion on himself was to be larger than life. Only those who were quiet and tried to remain unnoticed tended to be noticed.

He didn't try to steer the conversation round to the topic that interested him, figuring he would do that later if this technique failed. Instead he tried to understand who the characters in town were and what were the tensions.

If the conversation strayed towards asking him for personal details he provided only the basics, then veered the chatter towards other subjects, although he didn't balk from giving his name. He'd retained his parents' surname and he doubted anyone would remember a Temple Kennedy.

By the time people started drifting away he had made many friends, none of whom would remember him in the morning. But although he had gathered a more rounded picture of the town than Kate had provided, it didn't give him much hope of uncovering, in two days, what had happened when Hank went to see James Merritt.

The promise of work was attracting men to town, and sometimes it was available and sometimes it wasn't. The workforce was therefore itinerant and people leaving or arriving was a familiar sight.

Whoever had killed James Merritt could have arrived that day, then left town without attracting attention. Even if Temple found clues leading to the culprit, in the limited time he had left it was unlikely that he would be able to track him down and capture him.

Temple therefore put his hopes of solving the

killing on its having a specific reason. So he was relieved when the saloon quietened and the few people left started griping about their woes. He was sitting at a table with four men when the conversation drifted naturally to discussing Kate's husband George Fowles.

'He's starting to recover his grip again,' one man said. 'You want work, you have to get on his right side.'

Supportive muttering came from around the table so, in his guise as the newcomer to town who knew nothing, Jim shrugged.

'Who's George Fowles?' he asked.

'Let me explain how this town works,' his inebriated friend said. He moved the empty whiskey glasses around the table making everyone smile and shuffle on their seats, as if this was a common tale that they enjoyed. When he'd created a line of glasses down the centre of the table he sat back. 'That's the creek with the town to the south. That's Fowles's territory.'

'I didn't know someone owned that much land.'

'He doesn't,' another man said, pointing at various glasses as if they were well-known landmarks. 'But he doesn't need to as he owns the depot. The town and the south are filled with recent arrivals and they work with him and support his ways.'

'But to the north,' the first man said, 'it's wide-open spaces and ranches and they united behind

James Merritt. Slowly James was spreading his influ-
ence and he'd have rivalled George one day, but
then George got his brother-in-law to shoot him up.'

Everyone chuckled and licked their lips, showing
that they'd discussed this matter before.

'George wouldn't do that,' one man said. 'Hank
had his own reasons to kill James.'

'George had bigger reasons,' a second man said.

'He did,' a third man offered, 'but James's death
is the one thing that's gone badly for George. It'll
take him time to distance himself from his murder-
ous kin.'

Temple listened as what was clearly a familiar
argument developed. Sadly, throughout the debate
nobody seemed to doubt that Hank had killed
James; they just disagreed about the reason why.

When the conversation started listing grievances
against George's rangers, something that suggested
they were doing a good job, Temple interrupted.

'So if there's a feud between the Merritt and
Fowles families,' he said, 'did James's death end it?'

'Nope,' several men said before one man carried
on the story.

'It'll have started it. James's brother Emerson is
due back in town for the killer's hanging. Then he'll
stay and he won't stand for no more of this ranger
nonsense.'

Everyone chuckled as they contemplated a possible escalation of trouble. Then, with that animated

48

debate concluded, the conversation turned to a vigorous discussion about who served the best whiskey in town.

Temple joined in with the chatter, making no effort to leave and so showing he hadn't been overly interested in the conversation about town politics and rumours.

When the night's revelry was over everyone wandered outside. Temple expertly separated himself from the rest of his new-found friends and headed out of town. He judged that in the few hours he'd been here he'd learnt enough to give him several avenues of investigation to explore over the next two days, so he was in good spirits when he arrived at Hank's home.

Kate had wanted him to stay at her house, but he preferred to sleep here. This let him come and go as he pleased and, in an odd way, it brought him closer to the man he was trying to save.

When he drew up outside the darkened house, despite his tough mission he was looking forward to having an untroubled sleep for the first time for a while. But as he walked towards the door he had a feeling that something was wrong.

He wasn't sure what it was, but he stopped and stood poised, listening. Then a creak sounded as the door opened a fraction.

'Temple,' a voice urged through the gap, 'get in here.'

'Who's that?' Temple asked, struggling to place the speaker.

'It's me, Luther Duval.'

Temple winced. He'd last seen Luther in Big Springs after he'd killed the kid.

'What are you doing here?' he asked as he walked inside.

'I'm in big trouble,' Luther said in the darkness. 'And I need your help or we're both doomed.'

CHAPTER 5

Temple considered Luther by the light from the fire he'd lit, having judged that acting naturally was his best option to avoid drawing attention to the fact that he had an unwanted guest.

'What happened to the others?' he asked.

'The last few weeks have been terrible,' Luther said with a shiver, despite the fire that was warming the room. 'Cad was the first. He was all cut up about the kid getting killed. He got drunk and shot his mouth off. Some men followed him out of the saloon and made him pay.'

Temple shook his head at the irony of Cad achieving without trying what in his darkest days he had wanted to happen to him.

'And Burton?'

'That's when it got really bad. Bear Creek posted a bounty on our heads. Bounty hunters chased us everywhere. They were relentless. We split up to confuse them, but they followed him and shot him up.'

'That was tough on Burton. He didn't kill nobody.'

'I know,' Luther said. 'So you can imagine what they'll do to me. I've lost my money, my horse, everything. Now they're closing in.'

Temple noted the desperation in Luther's eyes and so he didn't ask the unsubtle question of whether that bounty named him.

'How did you find me?' he asked, settling for a better way of finding answers.

'I heard you were heading this way. I figured you were returning to your home town, so I sneaked on to the train.' Luther flashed a smile. 'Nobody knows about you. The bounty hunters are looking for only three people, but they reckoned the third one was Cad.'

'I'll help you,' Temple said, speaking in a low tone to disguise his relief. 'But keep your head down. If they find you, you're on your own.'

Luther had been nodding, but the last comment made him narrow his eyes.

'I've had enough of running. If they come for me, I'll make a stand, and I expect my friends to stand with me.'

Temple gave a brief smile. 'Let's hope it doesn't come to that.'

Luther's stern posture suggested that the obvious ultimatum on his mind was that if Temple didn't defend him he would reveal that Temple had been an accomplice in the tragic robbery. Then he leaned back against the wall and closed his eyes.

'I gave up on hope a long time ago,' he murmured. His head flopped down so that his chin rested on his chest. He began snoring.

Temple found him a blanket. Then, since it was too late to do anything else today, he rolled up in a blanket in front of the fire and watched Luther while trying to feel pity for his predicament. Temple had been through his own personal hell, but now that he had a purpose he'd come out of it.

Luther was about Temple's age, but his hair was greyer, suggesting that he had suffered more. Worse, he had no chance of redemption. Then again he deserved it; he was the kind of man who probably wouldn't take an opportunity if it came his way.

'But can I take my chance?' Temple asked himself before he slipped off to sleep.

'Anybody in there?'

The voice broke Temple out of his sleep and he found to his surprise that it was light. Luther was sitting bolt upright, his eyes wide with shock, showing that he expected the worst.

Temple ran the words that had interrupted his sleep through his mind. To his relief he recognized the voice. He gestured for Luther to calm down.

'He's not trouble,' he whispered before he raised

his voice. 'I'm coming out, George. Wait a minute.'

He hurried outside before George Fowles could come in, but he found that the major was sitting astride his horse while looking around. Temple couldn't tell whether that was because he suspected someone else was here or because he was uncomfortable about seeing him.

'Kate extends her offer for you to dine with us,' George said, his clipped tone hinting that this wasn't his reason for coming.

'I will if I get the chance,' Temple said, 'but my only aim is to free Hank and I need to spend my time doing that.'

'In that case I can offer my help.' George reached back to a saddle-bag and produced an unfolded blue jacket similar to his own. 'I'd like you to join the Rangers.'

Temple tipped back his hat in genuine surprise.

'I'm grateful for the offer, but I certainly won't have enough time to do that.'

George dismounted and came towards him, making Temple veer him away from the house in case Fowles detected that Luther was there.

'You won't have any duties other than freeing Hank, although I hope you can inspire my other recruits. Most of them are young and they would benefit from guidance from someone with integrity.'

Temple gulped and cast a guilty glance at the house.

'Kate speaks too highly of me.'

'Your modesty sits well with me. But you can't continue to ask questions anonymously in Prudence's saloons. People talk and before long your identity will become common knowledge.' George smiled. 'We have eyes and ears everywhere.'

'If you've learnt that, you may know that I learnt some interesting things about your fraught relationship with the deceased man. That's made you unpopular with some people and becoming a Ranger could ensure I find out nothing.'

'The death of a business rival who didn't support the Rangers has caused concern.' George shrugged. 'But then again joining a high profile group that annoys some of the factions here could reveal the truth.'

Temple set his hands on his hips, searching for a way to refuse so that he could investigate in his own way. He couldn't find a response, so he looked George in the eye and asked the only question that concerned him.

'Between you and me, who do you think killed James Merritt?'

'I don't know,' George said in a forlorn voice. 'About the only answer that makes sense is the one that can't: that it was Hank.'

'The evidence against him doesn't sound strong. From what I've heard people are convinced it was him more because of your feud with James than because of anything he did.'

'Or more likely it's because Hank was a Ranger. A group that keeps the peace frightens some, and the man it worries the most is Sheriff Simmons. With him achieving a conviction he has reasserted his authority and dampened my dreams that one day we may achieve what the Texas Rangers have.'

'I understand.' Temple kicked at the ground as he considered, then he sighed. 'So you're saying, if I join you I'll delight some and annoy others, and that might shake out the truth about what happened to James?'

'That's my offer.'

Temple held out a hand for the jacket. 'In that case I'm your newest Ranger, Major Fowles.'

George handed over the jacket followed by the coiled loop of a six-shooter and holster.

'You're welcome, Ranger Kennedy,' he said.

'So you're now working for me?' Temple said, eyeing the stiff-backed young man who only yesterday had held a gun on him at James Merritt's house, but who was now to be his deputy.

Abe Harris nodded. 'George reckons I'll learn from your expertise.'

'I'm not sure I have any of that. I intend to trust your judgement.'

This statement made Abe relax. 'I'm sorry about what happened yesterday. I didn't know who you were.'

Temple smiled. 'Don't worry about it. You weren't to know and as Major Fowles said, you dealt with me fairly.'

'Obliged,' Abe said.

With this subject discussed, the two men headed off for their first patrol. They rode in silence, but Temple judged it was a comfortable one and that let him think through how he could turn this new situation to his advantage.

They rode on to town and down the main thoroughfare at a steady pace. Temple followed Abe's lead in nodding to the people who acknowledged them, while watching those who didn't, but nobody appeared to be up to mischief.

Afterwards they circled round the south side of town and visited several shorter roads. Then they made a lengthier consideration of the depot where most of the buildings, as well as the crates and boxes that were stacked outside them, carried George's name.

Again there was no sign of anyone seeking to cause trouble, so they went back down the main road, this time on the other side, and then out of town to skirt around the north side.

Ultimately this route took them back to where they'd started, and so they embarked on a second pass along the same route as before.

Temple said nothing as they patrolled. He figured that Abe was the experienced man, so he should use the opportunity to become familiar with the problems he had to deal with in the hope that he would get a hint of who caused the trouble. But as the morning wore on and they did nothing but greet people, time began to press on him.

'Is it usually this quiet?' he asked.

'During the morning it is,' Abe said. 'It gets livelier in the afternoon and then more hectic at night.'

'I can't wait that long for something to happen. George told you why I joined, didn't he?'

'Sure. And before you ask I have no idea who killed James Merritt if it wasn't Hank.'

'Do you reckon the murder might have something to do with the disagreement between James and George?' Temple waited until Abe shrugged. 'Then the Rangers?'

'Not sure how it could be that either.'

'Then tell me about the Rangers,' Temple said, searching for a way to probe for information.

'George formed us last year to protect his interests at the depot. But people didn't like him turning a blind eye to trouble outside the depot. So six months ago he extended our work to cover nearby businesses, and when that went well, to cover the whole town.'

'And now not everyone agrees with that?'

'James didn't and he gathered others who had a problem, mainly on the north side of the creek, but we had a few successes and that quietened everyone.

Now it's only the troublemakers who don't like us, and Sheriff Simmons.'

'What was your last success?'

'Miles Shaw and Richard Cartwright, two good-for-nothing varmints who used to work for James. I reckon he only kept them on to annoy us. We stopped them three nights ago when they got drunk and roared through town. Simmons only kept them for a night. I reckon he treated them leniently.'

Temple drew his horse to a halt and waited for Abe to stop and turn.

'Where are they now?'

'They're staying in one of James's properties, but they had no reason to kill their boss. Nobody else would employ them, and they've stayed out of trouble since we arrested them.'

'If you want to root out trouble, you don't wait for it to happen while making a patrol that's so regular everyone knows your routine. You try to think like the troublemakers, then work out what they're planning to do.'

Abe accepted the suggestion with a nod.

'Their place is a mile on,' he said, pointing, 'but we have to be careful. We're not lawmen and George won't stand for us breaking his rules.'

'Then it's a good job he didn't tell me what they were.'

Abe's eyes widened with alarm until he saw that Temple was smiling.

With a greater sense of purpose than he'd felt so far today, Temple speeded to a trot as he headed down to the creek. The feeling that he might at last make progress grew when a quarter-mile from the house he saw that Miles and Richard were riding away from the house on a course that would take them out of town.

'I guess we're following them,' Abe said.

'Of course. It's just a coincidence that we're heading in the same direction as they are.'

Abe accepted this explanation with a brief smile. But five miles out of town he started fidgeting in the saddle, clearly concerned about abandoning his patrol to follow two men who were merely riding along, looking straight ahead, and giving no sign that they intended to cause trouble.

Another two miles passed before Abe eventually spoke his mind.

'This is far enough,' he said. 'By the time we get back to town we'll have abandoned our patrol for two hours.'

'If you're concerned, go back. I'm only here to seek out trouble, and it wasn't happening back in town.'

Abe looked back towards town, then to the men, and back again, but just as he was giving a reluctant nod the two men veered away from the trail and disappeared into a patch of cottonwoods.

'Now that was odd,' Abe said. He rubbed his chin.

'And maybe just odd enough for us to stay.'

They slipped off the trail and took a circular route towards the cottonwoods. This let them see that the riders hadn't emerged, but as they approached the trees they did see that three riders were heading towards town, perhaps providing a reason for the men's activities.

Temple and Abe tethered their horses to branches. Then Abe stood back to let Temple lead.

In a cautious manner they headed into the trees and took a slow route that avoided the trailing branches as they looked ahead for the men. When they first saw them, they weren't showing any signs of noticing that they were being approached, but unfortunately that was because their attentions were on the riders on the trail.

They were slipping to the edge of the trees while bent double with the air of men planning an ambush. Temple and Abe speeded up, not worrying about making noise, and they were thirty yards behind them when the men made their move.

They sprang out on to the trail.

'Get those hands high!' the men shouted.

Temple could see only thin slithers of the men's forms through the trees although he could hear consternation breaking out with horses whinnying and men shouting. He pointed at Abe, then to the side, directing him to take a route that would come out of the trees to the left of the men while he took a route to the right.

He didn't wait to confirm that Abe had taken his orders. He put his head down and ran.

He had to bat aside branches and his route turned out to be more overgrown than he'd hoped, so it took him over a minute before he closed on the edge of the trees. Worse, he'd had to veer away further than he'd wanted to and he'd lost sight of the men.

He stumbled out into the light and had to look around to get his bearings. Then, to his surprise, he found that the people he'd been aiming to capture were now the ones he needed to save.

One man had stayed on horseback while the other two had come down. These men were taking it in turns to pummel one of the would-be ambushers. The other man lay on the ground.

As Temple broke into a run, the rider raised a hand. After delivering another blow the fighting men stayed their hands to look up and watch Temple approach. A moment later they saw Abe.

'So,' the rider called airily, 'the Rangers are still riding to the aid of travellers in distress, are they?'

'That is our job,' Abe said, coming to a halt before him. He waited until Temple joined him before continuing: 'Even when the person being attacked is Emerson Merritt.'

'It's a pity the Rangers weren't so vigilant when my brother was being killed, or then again perhaps

Ranger Pierce was doing his duty when he killed him.'

'Hank Pierce,' Temple said, 'did not kill your brother.'

'Ranger Pierce certainly did.' Emerson turned his cold gaze on Temple. 'You look new and eager, but you'll soon wish you'd never joined the Rangers. I've come to see justice done. Then I'll complete my brother's work and end your reign.'

'If you want justice, you must want the right person to hang.' Temple glanced at the two attackers, both of whom were now crawling away in the hope that they could escape before they were noticed again.

'These two didn't kill him. They claim I owe them money. I've told them to collect from my brother.' Emerson flashed a cold smile. 'I can help them join him if they insist.'

'You won't do that while I'm a Ranger.'

'And who are you to make that threat?'

'I'm Temple, Hank's foster-brother, and I intend to keep his head out of a noose by finding out who really killed your brother. That means you can either help me or hinder me. The choice is yours.'

'I won't do either.' Emerson pointed to the horses and his two associates moved for them. 'I intend to stop you.'

CHAPTER 6

'We're still on duty,' Abe said as Temple moved to dismount outside the sheriff's office. 'We have to continue patrolling.'

'You patrol,' Temple said. 'Events will speed up now that Emerson is back in town, and I need to talk to Hank again. Everyone has told me their version of events and yet they keep leaving out small details, such as that it's possible Hank was on patrol when he found the body.'

Temple dismounted and went into the law office, but this time the reception he received wasn't an understanding one. Sheriff Simmons glared at him, then pointed at the door.

'It's not visiting time,' he muttered.

Temple winced and glanced down at his blue jacket.

'I'm here for only a few days. All I care about is proving that Hank is innocent. Joining the Rangers seemed one way to do that.'

'The law proved he was guilty.' Simmons folded his arms and leaned back in his chair, his firm gaze showing he was in the mood for an argument.

'I'm surprised you've sided with the Merritts. From what I've seen of Emerson he doesn't exactly support the law.'

Simmons frowned and rocked back down on his chair.

'He's back?'

'Just rode in, and he had two men beaten before he reached town.'

'James was a good man, but I can't say the same for his brother.' Simmons nodded to the door to the cells, and when he spoke again his tone was less truculent. 'See Hank, but do it quickly. I need to find out what kind of trouble Emerson's causing.'

With Simmons acquiescing Temple said no more and slipped through to the cells.

Hank was lying on his cot, his posture being the same as it had been yesterday. But unlike yesterday he looked up to see who was coming and he even smiled, showing Temple had give him hope.

'Any luck?' he asked when Simmons had left them alone.

'It's only been a day, but I'm making progress.'

'You only have the rest of today and tomorrow.'

'I know, but you have to trust me.'

'I do.'

Temple came up to the bars. 'So you need to do the one thing nobody else has done. Tell me everything. Tell me the rumours, what the Rangers did, the enemies you made, and the friends. I need to know because I reckon the answer to who really killed James Merritt is obvious, and yet nobody can see it.'

'The answer is obvious,' Hank said, coming to the bars.

Temple waited for him to continue, but having uttered those words Hank lost confidence and lowered his head.

'If you know something, don't keep it from me because it'll be dark in a few hours and then it'll be less than a day until they take you out of here.'

Hank looked up. 'I saw the killer, but I've never told anyone because they'd think I'd gone mad.'

'I won't,' Temple said, although he couldn't help but gulp on seeing Hank's eyes become troubled and hearing his breath quicken with the sudden onset of an emotion that could be strong enough to make him lose control.

Hank gripped the bars until his breathing calmed.

'When I went to James's house,' he said, 'the killer was standing over his dead body.'

'Did you see his face?' Temple snapped, now irritated that Hank was revealing such an important piece of information at this late stage.

'No, and I probably wouldn't recognize him if I saw him again. He was in the shadows with his head bowed and a hat covering his face. But I'd seen a man with his build lurking around down by the creek after dark.'

Hank met Temple's eye with a gaze that was again wild.

'What did you do?'

'I'm a Ranger. I tried to arrest him. He ran, so I fired at him. Then I realized my mistake.' Hank shrugged. 'I'd got it wrong. I wasn't seeing the killer, well, not directly. I shattered a mirror.'

'I saw the broken glass.'

'I didn't understand straight away what had happened, thinking he'd disappeared. I went to the body, then I saw the glass and realized I'd shot a reflection. But by then it was too late. Sheriff Simmons heard the shooting and he rushed in. The rest you know.'

'And the killer ran away?'

'He did. Simmons didn't see him or his shadow.' Hank laughed, although his blank eyes showed he did so without mirth. 'But then again the killer *is* only a shadow, a shadow I'd seen once before a long time ago.'

Temple waited for Hank to continue, but having revealed this much he'd lost confidence and again he had lowered his head.

'Who is he?'

Silence reigned for a minute before Hank looked up.

'The man who killed James Merritt,' he said, his voice small and barely audible, 'is the Prairie Man.'

'It's about time you turned up,' Luther grumbled when Temple returned to the house. 'I haven't eaten in two days.'

Temple tossed him the bundle of food he'd bought in town and then sat at the table to watch his unwelcome guest tear it open.

'I've been busy,' he said. 'I'm a Ranger now.'

Luther broke off from laying out the purchases on the floor to cast him an amused glance.

'When I found you, you were drinking yourself senseless and spoiling for a fight. Who'd have thought you'd work on the other side of the law?'

Temple frowned, noting that for once Luther was being subtle. He was reminding him that when they'd met his departure from Lucille had been troubling him, so in an odd way he'd helped him, even if that help had dragged him into even worse trouble.

'It's only for another day. Then everything changes.'

Luther brightened. 'We're leaving?'

'We could be. If I can find the man who really killed James Merritt, I'll stay for a while. If not, there's nothing for me here.'

Luther wolfed down a chunk of bread before he spoke again.

'Whatever you decide, those bounty hunters were

closing in and they won't take for ever to track me down.' He bit another mouthful and looked aloft as he became thoughtful. 'I'll need a horse and we'll need enough supplies to hole up somewhere for a while.'

Temple gave a slow nod while considering him with his brow furrowed.

'I'll need two horses.'

Luther narrowed his eyes. 'What you saying?'

'That if we leave together, we won't be alone.'

Temple waited for Luther's devious mind to provide him with a reason. When it did, it made him smile.

'If I had a foster-brother and he was locked up in a cell, I'd break him out.'

'We sure will.'

'I'm not helping you,' Luther spluttered, spraying crumbs. 'I have to keep out of sight.'

'We could argue about who owes the other the most and who could cause the other the most problems if he spoke up, but let's accept we're both in deep trouble and we need to help each other. I reckon you know more about how to plan a jailbreak than I do, so you can take care of that while I take care of getting us away.'

Luther joined Temple in sitting at the table and munched thoughtfully for a while.

'And if you can get him out the proper way?' he said.

'I'll help you leave without anyone seeing you and I'll give you the best possible chance of getting away with provisions, money, a horse, a gun. Then I never want to hear from you again.'

'It's a deal. I'll . . .' Luther trailed off as his gaze darted up to look over Temple's shoulder.

Temple swirled round to see the door swinging open to reveal Kate, her rounded stomach preceding her as always. They had been deep in conversation and he hadn't heard her approach. He jumped to his feet, but he was already too late to stop her seeing Luther, who was also acting guiltily by cringing down behind the table.

'I'm sorry,' she said, flustered. 'I didn't know you had company.'

'That's all right.' Temple turned to Luther. 'She's my foster-sister. You finish eating while we talk outside.'

His voice sounded stilted to his own ears, so when they were outside he wasn't surprised that she looked at him oddly.

'Who was that man?' she asked.

'He's a friend, shall we say?'

Kate accepted his guarded answer with a nod and joined him in a steady walk down to the creek. She bit her bottom lip pensively showing she wanted to ask him for more details, and he knew he'd struggle to find the right words to put her mind at rest.

He also owed her an explanation, so when they

reached the top of the bank overlooking the spot where fifteen years ago he'd nearly drowned, he stopped and faced her.

'I need your help,' he said, 'and your understanding.'

'You have it,' she said quickly, her tense tone confirming she had an inkling of the troubling news to come.

'I promised I'd get Hank out of jail, no matter what. And I will get him out whether that's by proving someone else killed James Merritt, or. . . .'

He left the thought unsaid, but she was already one step ahead of him. She threw a hand to her mouth in shock before she glanced back at the house.

'And that's why that man's here. I heard him saying something about getting him out and then you offered him some kind of deal.'

'I'd prefer not to do that, but there's no point proving Hank's innocence after they've hung him. We need more time and that's where you come in. If I break him out of jail, it'll make things tough for you, but you need to get your lawyer working on an appeal.'

'He is already. He's coming tomorrow to make one last plea for clemency. He probably won't succeed, but he surely won't if you and Hank are on the run. I don't want to lose a brother, and I certainly couldn't cope with losing two.'

'We're not related. You have only one brother, and this is the only way.'

She opened and closed her mouth, struggling to find a response.

'I won't try to stop you,' she said at last. 'But no matter how desperate Hank is, I don't reckon he'd want you to do this.'

'Hank doesn't know what he wants any more. I'm sorry to say this, but he's losing his mind. He's now got it into his head that he saw the killer.'

'Who?'

Temple frowned, now wishing he hadn't mentioned this.

'He must have had a bad dream or something,' he said, searching for a way to backtrack. 'The person doesn't even exist.'

'But who is he?' she demanded more insistently.

Temple shrugged and lowered his voice to alert her to the troubling answer to come.

'He reckons the Prairie Man killed James Merritt.'

Temple put on a wide smile hoping to placate her, but she uttered a pained murmur, then held out a hand for him to help her sit on the edge of the bank. She stared into the water.

'Could it have been him?' she murmured.

Temple tipped back his hat in bemusement as he sat beside her.

'I can't cope with you losing your mind too,' he said.

'I'm not. But I can't see how he could be right, even if it is a better solution than the ones I've come up with.'

'The Prairie Man was a tale your mother made up to stop us straying too far from home.'

For long moments she considered him, shaking her head.

'I'm so sorry,' she said. 'I thought you knew, but I guess you were still young when you left. Mother told me about it before she died. The Prairie Man was real.'

'He was a spectre.'

'In the tales she told us he was, but they were based on a real man. It was my fault. I heard her talking about him and she put my mind at rest by telling me it was a story, and later the story grew.'

'Who was the real man?'

'He was a troublemaker who harassed the home-steaders. He hid out of town and preyed on them, stealing food and clothes. He was always too fast and too devious for anyone to catch him. It took them a while to drive him off, but by then his crimes had worsened.'

He caught her change in tone and she looked at him with eyes that were brimming with tears.

'What crimes?'

'I'm sorry that nobody told you before, but he killed two homesteaders. . . .'

She gulped and was unable to continue, and

73

although Temple could guess the answer he had to hear her say it.

'Which homesteaders?'

She sobbed one long gasping cry, then fought back the tears before she replied.

'Your parents.' She put an arm around his shoulders. 'The Prairie Man killed your parents.'

CHAPTER 7

'I remember hearing about that,' Barney Watson said. 'Troubling business, troubling times.'

While Temple had been probing him for information about the formative years of the settlement, the old man had got every detail wrong, so Temple doubted that he remembered it. He looked at Abe to silently convey they should move on, a look that he'd had some practice in giving this afternoon.

Kate had given him a list of the original settlers who would have been here when the Prairie Man had terrorized the community. But most of the people were now dead or had moved on.

James Merritt had been amongst the early settlers, which added weight to the possibility of there being a connection. But of the nine who had been old enough at the time to know something useful, Barney was the sixth he'd questioned and, like the rest, he knew little.

Chasing the Prairie Man away was always something someone else had done.

He had only three men left to question, and Temple had mixed feelings about the likelihood of Emerson Merritt or Sheriff Simmons helping him. The other man was Walt Stone, who lived to the north of the creek where Emerson had now banned the Rangers from going.

Despite the lack of information, the little he *had* learnt had confirmed Kate's story.

Fifteen years ago a man had loitered around the settlement. A month later he had moved on, having escalated from thieving and general mischief to murder. Nobody knew who he was and nobody thought it likely that he might have returned fifteen years later to continue where he'd left off.

'Where next?' Abe asked when they were outside.

The sun was closing on the horizon, so Temple judged that they should question the remaining men in order of increasing difficulty. Walt would be next. Then they would try Emerson, after which he would report his findings, such as they were, to Sheriff Simmons to see if this information might sway him.

He didn't hold out much hope, and that hope diminished after they'd forded the creek and they were heading to Walt's house. They were being followed.

Two riders stayed several hundred yards back, watching them while not trying to come any closer. Abe reported that when he'd first noticed them he had reckoned there were four men, so Temple looked around in case others had veered away to outflank them.

He saw nothing, but when they closed on Walt's house they discovered the truth.

The riders had left to fetch Emerson, who now sat astride his horse fifty yards from the house, waiting for them. Flanking him were the two men they'd met on the trail earlier and when the two following men hurried closer Temple saw that they too had the menacing air of hired guns.

'You're on the wrong side of the creek,' Emerson said. 'The Rangers don't come here. Soon they won't go anywhere.'

The two hired guns snickered, but before Temple could speak Abe moved his horse on.

'You don't tell us where we can and can't go,' he said. 'If you don't want our help, we won't give it, but you don't decide that for others.'

Abe continued towards the house, but the riders moved to the side and blocked his way. Temple, now sure that a confrontation was inevitable, moved on to join Abe. He considered Emerson.

He waited until he had Emerson's attention then patted his jacket.

'Do you have a problem with me or with the

jacket?' he asked.

Emerson took a moment to reply, suggesting he was weighing up his answer.

'Your foster-brother killed my brother,' Emerson said at last, 'but then again neither of us was in town at the time and we weren't involved. If you want to talk to Walt personally, I won't stop you, but you will take off the jacket.'

Temple nodded, reckoning that Emerson either knew that Walt knew nothing or he was unaware of the nature of the questions he planned to ask; accordingly Temple watched him carefully as he asked his next question.

'When I'd finished with Walt, I'd aimed to ask you the same question, but I'll do that now.' Temple leaned forward in the saddle. 'What do you know about the Prairie Man?'

Emerson flinched, a barked refusal to answer that he'd clearly been preparing dying on his lips. He took several seconds to form another answer, giving Temple hope that, unlikely as it had seemed, the answer could lie with this formerly mythical man.

'I don't know why that would interest you.'

'I'm just rooting around looking for a way to save Hank,' Temple said, backtracking to avoid confirming that he'd seen Emerson's surprise. 'I've learnt that a man who once acted suspiciously here was seen when your brother was killed.'

'That's impossible. The Prairie Man left fifteen years ago. If that's what you're wasting your time doing, you'll never find anything that'll save Hank. Who else are you annoying with this question?'

'Everybody who was in town at the time. So if you have nothing useful to add, I'll check with Walt and then with Sheriff Simmons.'

Emerson gave Temple's jacket a significant glance.

'You can,' he said, 'but not as a Ranger.'

'I'm not. I'm seeing him as Temple Kennedy. I just happen to be wearing a jacket that I don't take off for nobody.'

Emerson snorted his breath through his nostrils while the men who were flanking him looked to him for directions. The men who had been following were now drawing up behind, closing them in, so Temple dismounted. Abe followed him and the two men sidestepped around the horses and strode briskly towards the house.

'Defy me, Temple,' Emerson shouted after him, 'and Hank's death will just be the start of your problems.'

With his head down Temple strode on. He heard the riders turn then approach. Two men dismounted while the other riders flanked them, calling out for them to stop. But Abe and Temple ignored them.

A hand landed on Temple's shoulder. Temple

shrugged it off. From the corner his eye he saw Abe attempt to do the same, but his assailant had gathered a stronger grip and Abe had to stop, then twist himself away from the hand.

Temple's follower grabbed his arm and tugged, halting him. Temple continued to look at the door ten yards away. Then, putting all the pent up force of his accumulated anger over the last day into his action, he spun on a heel and delivered a scything uppercut to his assailant's chin that sent the man reeling to the ground.

Temple didn't wait to see whether he got up; instead he confronted Abe's assailant. Abe and he were tussling, with the man trying to drag Abe away from the house. Temple carried out the tactic that had been tried on him.

He slapped a hand on the man's shoulder and spun him round. Then he delivered a straight-armed punch to his cheek that sent him staggering backwards into the corner of the house. The man moved to grab hold of the wall but he was moving too quickly and he tipped over to lie beside the house.

Temple turned to continue walking to the door, but then a shadow flittered across the ground a moment before a solid weight slammed into his back knocking him on to his chest.

The air blasted from his lungs as he lay pole-axed. A dazed part of his mind told him that one of the riders had leapt from his mount and pinned him to the ground, but he was too stunned to do anything about it.

Shouting went up and the thud of flesh on flesh sounded. With a shake Temple struggled to regain his senses, but then the weight lifted from him and someone grabbed his arm. He shook the hand off. Then he saw that Abe was trying to raise him.

He nodded to Abe, then let him drag him to his feet. He saw that three of the men were lying on the ground while the fourth had been shoved off him. With a glance at each other Abe and Temple moved in on this man. They slapped the man one way then the other before Abe delivered the blow that sent him spinning to the ground.

While standing over the prone man Temple looked up at Emerson, the sole man left for them to face who remained upright.

'And now,' Temple said, 'if it's all the same with you, we'll see Walt.'

The grounded men were getting to their feet while groaning; so, to avoid the distraction of a second round of their fight, Temple turned and with Abe at his side he headed to the door. He knocked but, seeing the men now closing in on him, he went straight in.

Two paces in he came to a sudden halt.

A prone body lay before the door. Blood had pooled around the head, bright and fresh, the scalp was matted and the skull was caved in.

'The Prairie Man got to him first,' Temple murmured to himself.

CHAPTER 8

The night was warm and it was one that Temple would enjoy normally, if it weren't for the fact this was the last one Hank might see.

Earlier, after the discovery of Walt's body, another confrontation had developed over who should report the news to the lawman. Emerson had been adamant it should be a friend of Walt's rather than the Rangers. Temple hadn't had the enthusiasm for another fight, so he'd relented.

He had returned to Hank's house, where he'd told Luther to take his horse and head into town. Now Luther would be examining the jailhouse to work out how they could mount a jailbreak.

When he returned, Temple would go into town to see Sheriff Simmons and find out whether the recent events had swayed him. Despite the situation moving on apace, he doubted that that would be so, and no matter how much he pondered he could make no progress in finding the solution to a mystery that felt as if it were tantalizingly close.

Emerson had been worried that the Prairie Man had returned and a new death supported this possibility. Emerson had clearly wanted to talk to Simmons alone, he being one of the few people in town who knew of the mysterious figure.

Temple didn't care what they decided, as by the time he could go into town Simmons would have had enough time to digest the new information and he might be able to shake out the truth. If not, he still had one more day in which to probe, and if that failed, he would have to put his trust in Luther's jail-breaking skills.

That thought made him look towards town. He couldn't see anyone approaching yet. He hoped Luther hadn't dallied in a saloon when they had plans to debate. Feeling irritated he walked along beside the creek to the old oak.

The tree was now old and in danger of toppling down the bank into the water, but it supported his weight when he leaned on it and looked north towards what was now Emerson's property.

A man was on the other side of the creek.

Temple shook himself, thinking that it was a trick of the light, but he hadn't been mistaken. One hundred yards away a man stood facing him with his lower legs hidden in the long grass, his coat ruffling in the breeze, his hat drawn down low, ensuring that his face remained hidden.

They stood silently considering each other. The man had no distinguishing features that would help Temple recognize him, but he had broadly the same build as most of the men he had bested earlier.

Temple placed a hand on the old oak, aiming to stand upright, but the feel of the wood evoked a memory that made his heart thud.

Fifteen years ago Hank had claimed he had seen the Prairie Man here. He had said so again recently. Temple hadn't probed him for details, but the situation was the same as the childhood tales had described.

A lone man stood there, watching, waiting.

It could be a coincidence, but it could also mean that the improbable was true.

Either way, the man showed no sign of changing the situation. So Temple took several paces to stand at the top of the bank. When this didn't encourage the man to move, he walked along it.

The man remained immobile even when Temple had moved 200 yards beyond him. Here, the creek was shallow and it could be forded easily. So with a last look at him, Temple headed down the bank.

The moment the man was out of sight Temple hurried. He slipped twice on the way down, but that only got him to the water more quickly. Then he waded through the creek, heedless of the loud splashing sounds he was making.

When he reached the other side he scurried on hands and knees up to the top of the bank before emerging in a calm way in case the other man was maintaining his own calm manner.

Temple wasn't surprised to see that he had gone, although when he looked around and he failed to see him he couldn't help but gulp. The low moonlight let him see for several hundred yards and he doubted that the man could have covered that distance in the two minutes he'd taken to cross the water.

Temple shook himself to fight off the growing spooked feeling then picked out the spot where the man had been. At a cautious pace he headed there, craning his neck to look around in case the man had merely lain down to hide in the long grass.

He'd seen nothing untoward when he reached a point that was roughly where his quarry had been. By glancing back at the oak he was able to orient himself. He moved twenty yards to the left where he saw trampled grass.

'You're no spectre,' he said, his relief making him speak aloud.

He took deep breaths, then examined the area. The grass had been flattened in a small circle. When he stood on that spot, he saw that the trampled grass trailed away and led back the way he had come.

For a moment he thought he might be looking at his own trail, but the tracks veered away to run beside the creek, past the spot where he'd climbed up. He looked further afield to a derelict building, one of the few on this side of the creek, 400 yards away.

The man must have sprinted to reach it, so he had probably been trying to create the illusion of disappearing to spook him. Confident now Temple followed the trail, walking in the man's footsteps.

Closer to the house he swung away so that he could circle in towards the building while seeing along the creek. He confirmed that the man hadn't gone to ground down the bank.

He stopped twenty yards from the house. It lacked a roof and the front wall had fallen in, letting him see the interior.

The mound that the front wall had created when it had fallen over wasn't high enough to hide his quarry. As the next derelict house was a few hundred yards on and that was in an even worse state, he had to be hiding around the back or behind the side wall.

'Stop playing games,' Temple called. 'Come out and we can talk.'

Silence greeted him. When that had dragged on for a while Temple walked round the building towards the far side. He took a route that would leave the man nowhere to hide even if he were being clever in mirroring Temple's movements on the other side.

The side came into view and then more of the grass behind the building as he moved to the back. He was two paces away from being level with the back wall when the man stepped out to face him.

He adopted the same posture as earlier, but this time Temple was only a few yards away and he could see the lower part of his face. His features were familiar. The man raised his head and Temple looked into the eyes of the Prairie Man.

'Emerson?' Temple said.

'Who else?' Emerson said, moving towards him.

It was only when he spoke that Temple broke out of the spell the bizarre situation had cast over him. He noted that Emerson was taller than the man he'd seen earlier and his coat was longer.

Rustling sounded behind him and he turned to see two men standing up from where they'd been hiding in the long grass, while from the corner of his eye he saw two more men move past Emerson. None of them was dressed like the man he'd seen earlier, but he did recognize them as being the men he'd bested outside Walt's house.

'Where's the other one?' Temple said.

'There's just us,' Emerson said, 'and you're about to find out how big a mistake you made when you defied me.'

Emerson gestured and the four men moved in with determined paces and with their arms held wide.

Temple swirled round, looking for an escape route, but the men had surrounded him. So he waited for them to come to him.

They couldn't all attack him at once, so one man stepped forward, swinging back his fist. Temple didn't wait for his assailant to act: he thrust his head down and charged him. He hit him in the stomach with a leading shoulder and carried him backwards for several paces before the man lost his footing.

Before the man hit the ground Temple turned and delivered a backhanded swipe to the nearest man that rocked him back on his heels. Then he kicked the legs out from under the next man, knocking him to his knees.

The fourth man was barging between these two men to reach him, but Temple ignored him, judging that his initial success was unlikely to last. He faced clear space that led on to the creek fifty yards ahead, so he ran for the bank, pounding through the grass.

He heard the others getting to their feet and chasing him while Emerson urged them on. The edge of the bank was a dark line, the water being out of view below; Temple reckoned he would have to act recklessly to stay one step ahead of his pursuers.

He put on a burst of speed, aiming to launch himself into the water from the top of the bank, but two paces from the edge his gaze alighted on the other side of the bank.

The Prairie Man stood there, watching him, as still

and silent as he had been on this side of the water.

The sight surprised Temple and he tripped. He tried to right himself and maintain his momentum, but his other foot slipped and he fell all his length. He slid over the side.

With his thoughts on the events of fifteen years ago he felt himself a child again, rolling down the bank in the dark. Stars swung around him as he sought to stop himself; this time he succeeded in fetching up on dry ground.

He shook himself and moved to clamber towards the water, but he was disorientated and his first step took him up the bank. He turned, but he was already too late. Two men ran into him and pinned him to the ground while the other two hurried down the bank.

He tried to throw them off, but they'd gripped his arms tightly and his jarring fall had weakened him. Two men stood back while the other two dragged him to his feet. They maintained firm grips, giving him no chance of escaping, as they escorted him to the top of the bank to face Emerson.

Temple glanced over his shoulder, but the Prairie Man had gone.

'Did you see him?' Temple asked.

'He ran,' Emerson said. 'He won't help you now.'

'He wouldn't. That was the Prairie Man.'

Emerson darted his gaze up to consider the terrain beyond the creek, then dismissed the idea with a shake of the head.

'Babbling nonsense won't save you.' Emerson looked at the men who weren't holding him. 'Enjoy yourselves, but not too much. I want him alive enough to appreciate the news of Hank's death.'

Emerson turned away as low chuckles sounded from the other four men. Then they moved in.

Light was streaming in through the shutters, but how much of the new day had passed, Temple didn't know.

Mercifully last night he had passed out while he was being beaten. That probably hadn't stopped his assailants from continuing with the blows. When he'd come to on the floor of Emerson's house, he had found it so hard to move he had thought he'd been tied up.

He'd lain there for several minutes flexing his muscles until he'd found that he was free, after all, but when he'd changed position a groan had escaped his lips. This had alerted Emerson.

He'd had him tied to a chair. He'd looked him up and down, sneered, and kicked the chair over. Then he'd left him.

Now he didn't feel any pain, but his sleep in a cramped posture on his side had numbed his limbs. The moment he started squirming the blood rushed back into his bruised arms and legs, forcing him to make another groan.

This time nobody came and so he took stock of

his situation. The room was small and unfurnished, with a single door leading to an inner room, and a shuttered window that was too high to look through even if he could right the chair.

By rocking himself he was able to shuffle the toppled chair round and confirm that behind him there was only a wall. There was nothing in the stark room that could help him get free, so he concentrated on working his way to the door. Inch by inch he rocked closer, pausing to gather his strength after every few movements.

The activity helped to free the tightness in his muscles and he learnt how to move himself more efficiently, so he speeded his progress. It still took him fifteen minutes to cross the room, so when he reached the door he'd already worked out how to open it. He looped the toe-end of his boot against the base then swung round, prising open the door.

After a full turn he moved to direct the chair into the next room, but then he winced on finding that Emerson was sitting quietly on the other side of the door. A small round table was at his side on which rested a ewer of water and a half-eaten plate of fruit.

'I find that to make defeat really hurt,' Emerson said, 'a small element of hope is essential.'

He gestured and two men arrived. They righted Temple's chair then carried him back into the room to place him beside the window. This time Emerson followed him in with his chair and sat. Another man brought in the table and his meal then left them alone.

Emerson considered him with his legs crossed, at ease and unhurried. Temple broke the silence.

'Why are you keeping me hostage?' he asked.

'So that you can't cloud the issue,' Emerson said. 'I will release you when I get the news that Hank has been hung, which will be in another few hours.'

'So you reckon I was making progress when I found Walt's body?'

'That discovery is unlikely to convince Sheriff Simmons that he has made a mistake.'

'You must want the right man to be punished for your brother's death.' Temple raised an eyebrow. 'Unless you have something to hide.'

Emerson took a sip of water. 'Do not try to rile me. Your only reward will be more pain.'

Temple didn't mind that if it gave him a chance of freedom, but Emerson appeared confident and in control as he watched him with a sly smile on his face. He reached over to the table and took an apple and a small knife.

Emerson peeled the apple concentrating on the task, presumably to draw Temple's attention to the apple and remind him that he hadn't eaten or drunk anything since last night. But Temple's attention was solely on the knife.

He looked away before Emerson noticed his interest.

'Perhaps I shouldn't rile you,' he said when Emerson took the first bite. 'Perhaps I should worry you.'

'You can't worry me,' Emerson said after swallowing. He placed the knife on the table. 'You are tied up in my house, guarded by my men, and nobody knows you are here.'

'I wasn't referring to my predicament. Last night you were lying in wait for me, but I came to you. Why was that?'

Emerson looked aloft as he considered. 'I saw the other man lurking around and you followed him, so we waited for you to come to us. But he wasn't the Prairie Man.'

'But what if you're wrong? What if the next time you're out after dark, he comes for you?'

Emerson spluttered over his last bite of apple, his reaction appearing genuine.

'Whoever was out there was just a man in the dark.'

'He was,' Temple said with as much assurance as he could muster. 'But then again so was the Prairie Man and you won't find out that it's really him until it's too late.'

Temple had hoped to worry Emerson into revealing something, but instead he jumped to his feet and stood over him with his fists clenched.

'I won't listen to any more of this madness. You are staying there until sundown. After that you can leave to see how much they've stretched Hank's neck.'

Emerson waited for a reaction, but when Temple didn't provide one he turned and paced out of the room, slamming the door shut behind him.

Temple looked at the wall, listening to his footfalls recede. Then Emerson barked orders. Men hurried to do his bidding and presently quiet returned.

Only then did Temple look at the table.

Emerson had left the ewer and plate. He craned his neck while rocking his chair round to see the rest of the table. He muttered an oath.

Emerson had taken the knife.

CHAPTER 9

After thirty minutes of careful and quiet shuffling movements Temple directed his chair to the table, but he only confirmed he had been right. The knife wasn't there.

Worse, the sun had now moved round to cast a thin slither of light over him, confirming that it was lowering. He was unable to work out the time, but it would be late afternoon and he had only a few hours before his efforts would end in failure.

Someone must have noticed he was missing, but with every passing minute his small hope receded that the Rangers might find him.

Kate would be busy in town with her lawyer and he hoped she had learnt about Walt's death as that provided an angle for her to explore. There was also the small possibility that Luther would use his own initiative to break Hank out of jail.

Temple shook his head, finding that Emerson had

been right; hopes and fears generated by dwelling on the unknown were crueller than the beating he'd had last night.

To stop his mind dwelling on such matters he again looked at the table. He nudged it making the ewer and plate rattle. Then with a smile to himself he hooked the toe of his boot around a table leg.

The plate was earthenware and therefore soft and unlikely to be useful, but the ewer was stoneware with a salt glaze, and sometimes glaze produced sharp fragments.

He dragged his foot to the extent of his reach making the table wobble. The noise he would make if he were to topple it would bring retribution. He was wondering whether to risk it when he heard conversation and then movement in the adjoining room.

He couldn't tell what was being discussed, but the conclusion came when men headed outside. He didn't know whether everyone had left, but he used the opportunity to wobble the table again. The ewer toppled, rolled, then fell off the table to smash on the floor.

The crash had sounded loud in the small room, but long moments passed without anyone coming to investigate. So he toppled his chair so that he could lie on his side and reach the shards.

Presently the bustle of riders moving away sounded and then footfalls approached as someone returned to the house. Temple judged that only one man, presumably Emerson, had stayed, but he didn't come to see him.

Temple got to work. Working behind his back, it took him several attempts to get his fingers around a piece that was sharp enough to cut the rope.

The piece felt comfortable in his hand and he worked efficiently, making him feel that his bonds were loosening. But then the shard broke and it took him an infuriating length of time to find a second piece.

The next hour was fraught. The thin stream of sunlight moved across the room, getting fainter.

In the rest of the house it was silent, although Temple felt sure Emerson would be able to hear his deep breathing as he strained to use the shards of pottery.

Working with increasing desperation as the sunlight took on a reddish hue, he scraped at the rope around his wrists. His breathing was becoming ragged as he faced the possibility that he wouldn't get free in time when with a sudden lurch the rope parted.

He swung his hands round to the front of the chair and stared at them with joy before he got to work on his legs. Gaining freedom took him but a few minutes, then armed with the small shard he shuffled to the door. It was still silent beyond, so he hurried to the window.

He opened the shutters and the sight of the outside bathed in dusky redness gave him renewed hope. The sun was below low cloud and still several widths away from the horizon. Provided he could slip out of the window unseen and get to a horse, he would reach town before sundown.

He had nothing to say to Sheriff Simmons that would ensure Hank's freedom, but he'd face that hurdle later. As he moved to leave, the door behind him creaked then swung open.

Temple swirled round to see Emerson standing in the doorway.

'It's sundown,' Temple snapped. 'I'm leaving.'

'Go,' Emerson murmured, his voice weak, an ironic smile on his lips. Then he keeled over on to his front.

Temple hesitated, torn between not questioning his luck, or finding out what had happened. Then he saw the dark stain on Emerson's back and the gleam of the protruding knife.

He hurried to Emerson's side and looked out into the room beyond, seeing no sign of anyone.

'Who?' he asked.

'Didn't see him,' Emerson croaked. 'He sneaked up on me. But we both know who it was.'

Emerson coughed and his breath came in short, shallow bursts.

Temple turned him on to his side so he could look up at him.

'Tell me,' he urged.

Emerson struggled to form the words, his mouth opening and closing soundlessly. He tried to say the phrase twice, but Temple got his meaning before he uttered the words aloud.

'The Prairie Man,' Emerson murmured.

His breathing slowed and he lay quietly. Temple didn't wait for him to die. The sun was lighting up the room with what could be its last rays of the day.

He had no choice but to hurry outside, where he saw no sign of the man who had killed Emerson, so he commandeered Emerson's horse and within minutes he was galloping back to town.

The low sun cast a long shadow to his side as he hurried on, willing the shadow to survive. The bruises and cuts that had pained him all day no longer seemed important as he headed down to the creek then forded it.

He passed Hank's house confirming, as he had expected, that his own horse had gone. Luther presumably had made good his escape.

He surprised himself by wishing him well. Luther had done a terrible thing and one day he would pay the price. If he were lucky, he would get a chance for redemption, as Temple had.

This thought spurred him on, but despite his speed his shadow was dying when the town opened up to him and it was with some relief that he noted that the main road wasn't especially crowded tonight.

The hanging wasn't to be a public affair, but he still expected a crowd to gather. As it was, only a small delegation stood outside the sheriff's office. He was thankful to see that Kate was amongst them.

She saw him riding down the road. She put a hand to her mouth in relief, then beckoned him on.

'You've been hurt,' she said as he drew up.

He dismounted in a hurry then grabbed her elbows and looked into her eyes.

'No time to explain. How long have we got?'

'Possibly another half-hour, maybe more,' she said responding to his silent plea for urgency by speaking quickly. 'Judge Canby is here. He's talking with our lawyer. It sounded as if there was no hope, but maybe if you have something to tell them there might still be time.'

She raised her eyebrows, her earnest gaze imploring him to offer her some assurance.

'I do. I hope it's enough. But there's no time to explain. I need your lawyer with me when I see Sheriff Simmons.'

'Understood,' she said. She gripped his arms in relief then turned to the door.

'And whatever happens,' Temple said as he joined her, 'please accept that this was the only way.'

She stopped to look at him, her eyes opening wide as she perhaps caught an inkling of what he might have to do, but he breezed past her to the door. Inside Simmons, the lawyer and Judge Canby stood

101

around Simmons's desk, their expressions and postures relaxed as they discussed what to them was business, although they became sterner on seeing who had entered.

'These interruptions aren't helping anyone,' Simmons said.

'Temple has news,' Kate said, keeping back to let Temple approach them.

'That won't change anything. Walt's death was terrible, but it has no bearing on this case. The moment I can move on from this, I'll search for Walt's killer.'

'The death of one of the first batch of settlers,' Temple said, 'could be connected to James Merritt's murder. There's not many of you left now.'

Simmons winced before he glanced at Judge Canby for aid.

'I'm sorry about your situation,' Canby said, using a softer tone than Simmons had managed, 'but in this Simmons is right. Hank had his chance in open court, and for me to seek a postponement would require compelling new evidence.'

Temple nodded. 'Emerson Merritt, another of the early settlers, reckons there's a connection. The Prairie Man has returned.'

Simmons made an odd squeaking noise that must have been an instinctive reaction as he then coughed to cover his discomfiture while he sat on the edge of his desk.

'I've never heard of this man,' Canby said.

'Few have,' Simmons said, rubbing his chin while looking distracted. 'He was a troublemaker here fifteen years ago. He left.'

'Troublemaker,' Temple said, 'isn't how I would describe the man who killed my parents.'

Simmons frowned, looking for a moment as if he might seriously consider Temple's idea, but to Temple's irritation this revelation made Canby shake his head.

'I can see why you want to link these personal tragedies, but I must decline to consider this matter unless you can provide me with substantial proof.'

Temple took a deep breath. 'I have it. Emerson Merritt has been killed.'

'That can't be the Prairie Man's fault,' Simmons said.

'I agree,' Canby said. 'You're listing worrying incidents that Simmons must investigate, but you haven't provided a single link between this man whom nobody has seen for years and the murder we're dealing with today. Speak now, or I will move on.'

Everyone looked at Temple, who considered the various scraps of evidence, half-truths, and hints of events he'd gathered. But in the moments left to him he couldn't connect them to provide the proof that he was sure was within his grasp.

He waved his arms as he struggled to find something to say. But seeing no other option, he stilled. He returned to the thought that had been at the back of his mind ever since he had first heard that Hank was in jail, the thought that had always been his last desperate option if all else failed.

He would give his own worthless life to save Hank's worthwhile one.

He flashed what he hoped was a comforting smile at Kate then faced Judge Canby.

'Would a signed confession from the man who really killed James Merritt be enough to postpone this hanging?' he asked.

'It would,' Canby said, blowing out his cheeks in bemusement as he contemplated the unlikely possibility of this being delivered.

'In that case, I'll oblige,' Temple said. He walked around Simmons's desk and picked up a sheet of paper.

'Who will be providing it?' Simmons asked as Temple searched for a pen.

'I will,' Temple said sitting. 'I am the killer. I killed James Merritt and then I moved on to killing Walt Stone and Emerson Merritt. So hang me instead.'

CHAPTER 10

'This is preposterous,' Simmons spluttered as Temple continued to ignore him and write out a short statement admitting to all the recent killings.

'Listen to Simmons,' Kate said, leaning over the desk to face him. 'It's a brave gesture, but it won't work.'

Temple kept his head down and continued scribbling, forcing her to turn to the lawyer and demand that he talk sense into him, but when someone moved in to stop Temple, it was the judge.

Canby planted a firm finger on the edge of the paper, but he didn't drag it away: he merely let Temple know that he could stop him if he chose to.

'As the circuit judge,' he said, 'I will try any case presented to me, and a confession written in this manner and in these circumstances won't sway me.'

'When a man says he did it, you have to listen.'

'I do. But I listen to what he's really saying, and

you are saying you care for Hank so much you are prepared to die in his place. Don't waste his last minutes on this futile gesture. Go to him and make your peace.'

Temple resumed writing to avoid the judge's searching gaze. Canby watched him then shook his head sadly and stood back to let Simmons face him.

When Temple had finished the closing sentence of his short statement he signed it, then pushed it across the desk towards Simmons.

'There's no evidence that you've done anything wrong,' Simmons said without looking at the paper.

'Ranger Harris saw me arguing with Emerson Merritt yesterday,' Temple said.

'More people saw Emerson arguing with Miles Shaw and Richard Cartwright after he'd had them beaten. They'll be the first people I go looking for.'

Temple firmed his jaw, unwilling to accept this less mysterious explanation for what had happened to Emerson.

'Look at me first. I got worried that Emerson would work out that I killed Walt, and so I killed him. I killed Walt to make you think that James's killer was still at large.'

With Temple growing in assurance as he warmed to his bogus confession, Simmons narrowed his eyes, appearing to pay serious attention for the first time.

'This is becoming interesting,' he said. He set his hands on his hips. 'But Hank isn't being hanged for those crimes, and James Merritt died long before you arrived in town.'

'So you thought. I came here secretly and killed James, but I didn't know Hank would find the body and get arrested for it.'

Simmons sighed and cast an exasperated look at Canby, who shrugged then looked to Kate.

'Please stop now,' she said. 'You've tried everything you possibly could. I'll never forget that, but now it's time to accept it's over.'

'It's not,' Temple said standing and holding out his confession to Simmons. 'I was there. I saw the blood-soaked body lying before the broken mirror. How would I know that if I didn't do it?'

'You spoke to Hank. Then you broke into James's house.' Simmons gave a thin smile. 'Despite what the Rangers think, nothing passes me by.'

'Except,' Temple shouted as Canby chuckled in agreement, then moved to join Simmons in making for the jailhouse, 'for the one detail that Hank doesn't know, but is known only to you and me.'

Simmons stopped. 'Which is?'

'The reason why the mirror was smashed. I fired bullets into it when I saw the Prairie Man, except he escaped.'

Simmons swirled round, proving that Temple's gamble had worked. Hank hadn't told anyone but him what he'd seen in the mirror, and yet the sheriff's reaction showed that he too had seen

someone else there that day. For long moments
Simmons considered Temple.

'You are under arrest for the murder of James
Merritt, Walt Stone and Emerson Merritt,' he said,
his voice almost too low for Temple to catch the
words, making Canby look at him in puzzlement.

'What did you say?' he demanded.

'I am arresting Temple, so I suggest you postpone
the final stage of Hank's sentence until we have considered this further.'

Canby bristled and after glaring at Simmons with
his arms folded for several moments he beckoned
for him to join him in a corner of the room. The
lawyer hurried over to join them, leaving Temple to
face Kate, who stared at him with a mixture of shock
and relief in her eyes.

'This won't work,' she whispered, 'and I don't
want it to.'

Temple offered a tentative smile.

'I would gladly die to save him. So don't worry
about me.' He raised a hand as she started to object.
'But I haven't lost my senses. I've earned Hank a
postponement and that gives us time to work out
what's happening. And it has something to do with
the Prairie Man and events here fifteen years ago.
Speak to people from back then. Find out the truth.'

'We have the Rangers. Now that we have a start,
my husband will get to the truth, and my lawyer will
tie this up in so many knots even Judge Canby won't

be able to untie them all.'

Her voice broke twice during her declaration, proving that her positive thinking was more to cheer him than because she believed it, but Temple didn't mind as long as she acted. Then there was nothing left to do other than to await the conclusion of Simmons's and Canby's deliberations.

'I'll sleep on this,' Canby said wearily when he came over. 'For now you'll join Hank in the jail-house. I hope you sleep well and are prepared to act more rationally in the morning or I'll lock you in a cell until you rot for wasting my time.'

Having made that statement of intent Canby went outside, closely followed by the lawyer. Kate gave Temple a comforting smile.

'Until tomorrow,' she said with a sniffle before she hurried out.

Temple watched her go, then faced Simmons, who shook his head and gestured for him to raise his hands. He frisked him, then moved him on to the door to the cells.

Simmons maintained a pensive frown as he manoeuvred him through the door and to a cell, choosing one that was two away from Hank's. A new occupant was in the cell between them, a snoring drunk.

Temple could tell that Simmons had a lot on his mind, but he resisted the urge to press home his advantage and force him to admit that more was happening here than he had previously admitted. He preferred to let the sheriff stew, to let him come to him.

Silently Simmons pushed him into his cell and locked it. Then the sheriff stood with his head bowed on the other side of the bars.

From the corner of his eye Temple could see Hank pacing his cell, clearly wondering what was happening, but instead of reassuring him he came up to the cell door and faced Simmons. Slowly Simmons raised his head. His eyes were sad.

'I never wanted it to end like this,' he said, his voice low.

'What do you mean?' Temple prompted when he didn't continue.

'Sentiment won't sway Judge Canby. He won't believe you. Hank will still die, except it'll be tomorrow rather than tonight.'

'He has to accept my statement.'

'Sadly for you he'll accept some of it. All you've done is make yourself the main suspect for killing Walt and Emerson. You'll follow Hank to the gallows all too soon.'

Simmons shook his head, sighed and walked towards the cell-block door. Defeated, Temple flopped down on to his cot.

'What have I done?' he said as the door slammed shut.

'What have you done?' Hank said from the end

cell, emotion making his voice high-pitched.

Temple fought down his disappointment to manage a tense smile.

'I've earned you a reprieve. Judge Canby is thinking some more overnight.'

Hank looked aloft, sighing with relief before he moved on to practical matters.

'Might he change his mind?'

Temple detailed the recent events, although he left out one crucial element. He explained that he'd been arrested on suspicion of being involved in Emerson's and Walt's deaths, not that he'd claimed that he'd killed them. He left the details of the Prairie Man to the end.

'There must be something behind those stories, after all,' he said, finishing his tale.

Hank sat back on his cot, his expression more relaxed than Temple had expected to see after providing him with an honest assessment that his situation was still dire.

'Just knowing there probably is an answer is a relief,' he said. 'All this time I thought I'd dreamt the sighting.'

'If you dreamt it, then I did too.'

'In which case we need to talk this through until we work out what's going on,' Hank said, his cheerful mood dying. 'Because if we can't figure it out, nobody else can, and I'm doomed.'

'Don't be downhearted. Kate and her lawyer will

do everything they can.' Temple considered, searching for another angle that might provide hope. He brightened, then lowered his voice. 'And don't speak of this again, but someone might break us out of here.'

'A jailbreak?' Hank spluttered.

Temple put a finger to his lips as Hank's outburst encouraged the drunk to let out a prolonged snore, then stir and try to throw off his blanket.

'Yes,' he said. 'When things were looking desperate, I got someone's help to break you out. I don't know where he is now, but I hope he's still working on that escape plan.'

'Then I can put your mind at rest,' the drunk said slurring the words. He sat up on his cot to gaze at Temple. 'I am still working on the plan to free him.'

Then, with a hiccup and a groan, Luther Duval rubbed his brow and flopped back on his cot to stare up at the ceiling.

CHAPTER 11

When Temple awoke first light was illuminating the bars in the door to the law office. He and Hank had talked long into the night, but they hadn't been able to make any sense of events.

They had tried to use Luther as a sounding board for their discussions, but a sore head and a greater concern for his own future had made him uncooperative.

They did learn that he had come into town to find a way to break Hank out of jail, but the lure of his first drink for weeks had been too strong. As usual, he hadn't been able to stay out of trouble and now he reckoned it was only a matter of time before Sheriff Simmons connected him to his past.

Temple reckoned Simmons was also the key to his and Hank's troubles, and he hoped the sheriff hadn't spent his time on checking out Luther and instead had investigated Walt's and Emerson's deaths.

'Are you awake?' Temple asked, peering at the darkened corner of the room.

'Sleep didn't come,' Hank said. He snorted a harsh laugh. 'The only thing worse than knowing you'll die when you next wake up is going through the experience twice.'

Temple tried to think of something to say that would cheer him, but his mind remained blank, so he sat with his back to the bars and watched the room brighten. Presently he heard movement outside as the day got under way and later someone started shuffling around in the sheriff's office.

Even if Sheriff Simmons had found something, Temple didn't expect that he would burst in with the news, so he waited quietly.

He'd been awake for an hour when Deputy Haynes came in to feed them. Hank left his plate on the floor while Luther wasted no time in tucking into his food. Temple took the plate but he also caught Haynes's eye.

'Is Simmons here?' he asked.

'Not yet,' Haynes said. He glanced at Hank. 'He's probably investigating what happened to Emerson.'

Haynes turned to go, but Temple halted him with a quick question.

'What does he think happened to him?'

Haynes didn't turn round immediately, being clearly reluctant to answer. Then he gave a small shrug as if he'd come to a decision.

'He doesn't believe you killed him, if that's what you're asking.' Haynes turned, his raised eyebrows inviting him to ask for more details, but having heard that Temple didn't want to hear any more. Haynes continued anyhow. 'The reason being that Emerson survived, but he could well be telling Simmons some interesting things.'

Haynes snorted a laugh at Temple's incredulous expression then headed to the door.

'Is that good news or bad?' Hank asked when he'd gone.

'I don't know,' Temple said. 'I guess it depends on what Emerson's telling him.'

Then there was nothing left to do but let the morning pass.

They didn't know when Judge Canby was due to present his verdict, so time dragged where every moment that passed provided a mixture of hope that something might be happening while bringing the moment of revelation closer.

When full light arrived, Temple marked time by listening to Hank's steady pacing back and forth, punctuated by occasional stops when a noise sounded in the law office. But when sounds of bustling industry came they were from the court-room on the other side of the office.

Temple couldn't help but view this as being a bad sign.

Scraps of a distant conversation came to him and

he strained his hearing to hear words or even recognize voices, but he couldn't discern anything. They were talking calmly though.

Hank paced his cell for around a hundred more times before the door from the courtroom opened. Only Judge Canby entered. He stood by the door and looked through the line of the cells at them.

He lowered his head before he moved on, the small gesture telling Temple everything he needed to know, but Hank stopped his pacing to await the answer.

'I will be leaving for Redemption City now,' Canby said.

'When?' Hank croaked, his voice small.

'At sundown.' Canby flashed an apologetic smile. 'But you had an extra day to make your peace. I hope you can use your last hours wisely.'

He walked past the cells, giving Luther a cursory glance. He stopped before Temple's cell.

'This is wrong,' Temple said.

'I decided on the rights and wrongs some time ago,' Canby said. 'I will return next month when I presume I will decide on the rights and wrongs of your case.'

'Wait!' Temple said. 'There has to be something else we can do.'

Canby moved back to the courtroom doorway, where he stopped. Then, with a heavy tread, he carried on through it.

A thud sounded as Hank slumped down on to the floor and put his head in his hands. Temple didn't want to burden him with his problems, but Canby's comment hadn't been lost on Luther, who edged closer to his cell.

'It sounds as if they've worked out who you are,' he said.

Temple shrugged. 'If Simmons lets you out of here before someone links us, I won't tell them about you.'

Luther sighed. 'It's the same for me.'

He gave Temple a pensive look, but Temple didn't make the request Luther must be expecting. When Luther had been arrested their plans for a jailbreak had been at an early stage. If Luther was released today, Temple couldn't expect him to help them out, especially when he'd relinquished his hold over him.

Luther offered a smile, perhaps acknowledging this before with a cough, he resorted to staring at the door to the law office, as if he could make Simmons appear by force of will alone.

The effort proved to be worthwhile as a half-hour after the judge had gone Simmons entered. He ignored Temple and Hank and opened Luther's cell.

'You slept it off?' he said.

'Sure,' Luther said, giving an innocent smile as he tried to appear as if he were a nobody who had just been unlucky in catching a lawman's attention. 'I'm

117

sorry I got carried away. I haven't had a job for a while. Then I got me one last night and I went loco. I won't cause you no trouble again.'

'See that you don't and we'll get on just fine.'

Luther glanced at Temple and winked. Temple returned a silent salute. Then Luther rolled off his cot. He walked sideways out through the door, looking at Hank with concern, but Hank was still sitting on the floor, lost in his own private misery.

His interest made Simmons look at Hank, but at that moment, with a sudden change of attitude Luther darted in. Simmons saw him coming and he stepped away but his shoulder caught the edge of the door, slowing him.

In a moment Luther was on him. Metal gleamed, catching a stray beam of light and dazzling Temple. He wasn't sure what he had seen and he leaned forward to watch the two men tussle. Even Hank looked up.

With surprising speed Luther wrapped a firm arm around the lawman's neck, then spun him round and dragged him backwards to press his back to his chest. Only then did Temple see what had happened.

Luther had thrust a knife up against the lawman's neck.

'Where did you get that?' Simmons muttered, speaking Temple's thoughts.

'Your deputy found a knife,' Luther said, leaning

over his shoulder to look into his face. 'But he should have looked harder.'

'And you should have just left.' Simmons shook his head in puzzlement. 'You're the first prisoner I've ever had who's tried to escape after I'd released him.'

'I'm not bothered about me. I've been listening to that one's story. He doesn't deserve to hang. Open his cell.'

Simmons didn't move at first, forcing Luther to encourage him by pressing the blade into his neck. Simmons winced as blood welled, but he did move on to Hank's cell.

'This is a bad move,' Simmons said as he selected the right key. 'You're making yourself as guilty as he is.'

'Or as innocent, lawman. Don't waste time coming after us. Get others to track us down while you investigate his case properly.'

'I don't act on your directions. I'll be coming for you, Billy.'

Luther cast Temple an apologetic look that acknowledged the fact that he had provided an alias then kept his attention on Simmons as he opened the cell. Hank bounded out and grabbed the ring of keys off the lawman.

'You coming?' he asked Temple.

'I guess so,' Temple said. 'We can't sort this mess out in here.'

'You'll get yourself into even more trouble if you run,' Simmons said.

Temple slipped out through the opening door and walked up to him, shaking his head.

'We won't. We'll just hole up, not cause no trouble, and wait until we hear that you've caught the Prairie Man. Then we'll return.'

Simmons said nothing other than to cast him an angry look, so Temple disarmed him. Luther frisked him with greater care than clearly he had been frisked. Then he used a long kerchief to gag the lawman.

While he was locking him away Temple went to the door. Through the bars he saw that the office was empty, but the deputy was just returning to the office after completing an errand. To get out quietly without bloodshed they would need care and good timing. He bided his time.

Hank joined him and he stood to one side of the door, waiting while Temple crouched down beneath the small window.

Sure enough after a few minutes the silence in the jailhouse concerned the deputy and he came to the door. Temple listened to his footfalls and counted down his approach so they could co-ordinate their assault.

The moment Haynes's form darkened the window bars, Temple threw open the door, causing the deputy to teeter in surprise. Fuelled by desperation, Hank burst out and grabbed Haynes then carried him backwards for several paces until both men fell to the floor.

Temple followed him out at a more sedate pace and stood over them, but Hank was seizing his chance for freedom and he didn't need any help to subdue the deputy. When Hank had disarmed him, he walked Haynes back into the jailhouse, where Luther put him in a cell two away from Simmons.

Hank found several short lengths of rope. While he and Luther trussed up the lawmen Temple raided Simmons's armoury for guns as well as gathering a few provisions. Then he stood by the window.

It was late morning and few people were about. Even better, three horses were at the hitching rail outside the office.

When Luther and Hank joined him they considered the scene and deemed that it was safe for them to leave. Luther volunteered to go out first, as he was the one who was in the least trouble and so would presumably attract the least attention.

He walked across the boardwalk in an unhurried manner and checked that the horses were ready to go. Then he casually looked up and down the road, as if he were undecided what to do today, before he mounted up.

He nodded to Temple and he and Hank came out, but they weren't as good at presenting a calm demeanour as Luther had been, and in short order both men leapt on their horses. Despite their haste,

Temple judged that nobody paid undue attention to them as they trotted away.

Hank rode with his head bowed and his hat drawn down low, but Temple risked looking around, figuring that his predicament wasn't well known. Nobody looked their way or followed them and the moment they reached open land they speeded up.

Only when they were riding alongside the creek did they slow and take stock of their situation.

'Why did you save me, Luther?' Hank asked, broaching a subject that had been on Temple's mind. 'You were only in there for a minor crime. Now you're in big trouble.'

'It's a long story,' Luther said, 'and maybe when we're safely holed up somewhere I'll tell it to you.'

'Whatever the reason, you're a good man.'

Luther coughed and cast Temple a sideways glance.

'You got that wrong, but we need to decide where we're going.'

'I reckon we need to put as many miles as we can between us and Prudence,' Temple said. 'But not so many that we can't find out what's happening back here.'

'I'd put that out of your mind,' Luther said. 'Give it a year, maybe longer, before you even think of finding out what's happened. Only time will make you safe.'

Temple gave a brief nod, accepting that others would now have to uncover the truth, but when he looked at Hank he was shaking his head.

'You two can keep going,' he said. 'I'm staying close to town.'

'You're hours from the noose,' Temple said. 'You can't risk it.'

'I can. I don't know what's going on here. Kate could be in danger too.'

Temple winced, not having considered that possibility.

'Her husband leads the Rangers. She'll be safe. You need to think of yourself for a while.' Temple waited until Hank started to shake his head. 'And our best chance is to stick together.'

Hank bit his lip as he sought a retort, but then he gave a brief and reluctant nod.

'All right. We move on, but only after I've seen her and explained what we've done.' He pointed ahead. 'After all, it is on the way.'

Temple didn't feel inclined to persuade him that this was the wrong thing to do, but to his surprise, when he looked at Luther he was nodding.

'You agree?' Temple said.

'We don't have a choice,' Luther said. He pointed back towards Prudence. 'We're being followed, after all.'

Temple turned in the saddle. A half-mile behind them three riders were moving in and several more were closing in from the sides, speeding to a gallop as they approached.

CHAPTER 12

By the time the three men were closing on Kate's house the pursuing riders were a hundred yards behind them. Worse, they were close enough for Temple to recognize them as Emerson's men.

Temple doubted they would be able to outrun them and with nothing but the open prairies beyond the house they had no cover to head for. Quick nods from the other two men confirmed they also thought that they had no choice. So they swung in through the gates in front of the house and leapt down to the ground outside the stables.

These and the house were the only two buildings here. They hurried to the house, but they had managed only a few paces when their pursuers started firing at them.

The distance was too great for accuracy and their shots were wild, but several clattered into the house and one smashed a window.

'To the stables,' Hank shouted.

Temple joined him in backtracking. Luther dallied, but the porch was thirty yards away and the stables ten. He joined them. As their spooked horses were spreading out and covering them no further gunshots came, letting them reach the relative safety of the building.

Temple confirmed that the large double doors at the front were the only way in. Then he stood to one side of the doorway while Hank took the other. Luther moved into the shadows, looking for a way up on to the short hayloft.

Now that they had good protection Temple looked out, to see that the men had dismounted. He and Hank laid down a quick burst of lead at the attackers, and this encouraged them to seek cover.

As Hank's and Temple's gunfire hurried them on their way at least four men scurried behind a buggy that stood square on to the stables. Another three men found themselves trapped in the open. They went to ground in the nearest cover of a depression, where they lay flat and out of sight.

Temple was on the side nearest the house and he saw no sign of anyone coming out to investigate. Since Kate was presumably still working with her lawyer to free Hank and with George perhaps patrolling with his Rangers, it was possible that the house was deserted.

This was fine with Temple, but getting away from Emerson's men wouldn't be easy.

'What do you want with us?' he shouted.

'You'll find out soon enough,' one man shouted. 'For now, you're not going nowhere.'

Temple tried further taunts to get more information, but he didn't get a response and, worse, their horses mooched off for a short distance. They could be reached in a few seconds, but the three men in the stables were so outnumbered that they stood little chance of laying down enough gunfire to get away unscathed.

They needed a distraction. Temple looked to Hank for ideas, but he returned a sorry shake of the head. Then he looked up to Luther. He had clambered up into the loft and was searching for a gap in the wood through which to see their attackers.

'I can pick 'em off from here,' he said, leaning back to face them. 'While you make a run for the horses.'

'But you won't get all of them,' Temple said, 'and besides, we're not leaving you here.'

'I never said you should. Just get my horse too and we'll get out of here while making them eat enough lead to make them think twice about coming after us.'

Temple was about to shake his head, but Hank caught his eye.

'It's a plan,' he said. 'And we have to do something before Kate returns.'

Temple glanced at Luther who nodded. He

looked to the house, picking out a route to their horses. They were eating flowers from baskets on the porch, so they'd have to cover thirty yards in full view from the buggy. Even with Luther's cover Temple reckoned they'd need plenty of luck. He looked for another possibility.

His gaze alighted on one of the stable doors. It had been moved to the side wall for repair. It was heavy and it wouldn't provide adequate protection from sustained gunfire, but it was bulky enough to mask their precise location.

He backed away to the door and picked it up, finding that he could just about lift it on his own. Even better, on the back a length of wood held the planks together; it was at the right height for him to rest it on a shoulder.

He looked at Hank, who glanced through the open doorway then hurried over to join him.

'Let's do this,' he said taking hold of the door, 'before I start thinking about how bad an idea it is.'

Temple nodded and when Luther signalled that he was in a good position, they manoeuvred the door to the side of the doorway.

'Wait until we've drawn their fire,' Temple said to Luther. 'Then give them hell.'

On the count of three they raised the door, ducked down to keep their heads below the top, and fast-walked outside. To Temple's delight they pounded on for five paces before a cry of alarm went up.

Someone shouted out that they needed to be stopped while someone else demanded they went back to the stables. They took advantage of the confusion and kept walking, and even better, they achieved a rhythm that let them speed up.

They'd halved the distance to the nearest horse when the shooting started. Lead whistled over the top of the door. Then a second shot sprayed splinters a few inches from Temple's hand. In an instinctive gesture he flinched his hand back and the temporary loss of support made the door plough into the ground and bring them to a grinding halt.

Luckily it also stopped the men firing as they awaited their next move. Luther gave them plenty to think about as he rattled gunfire at them. Shouted orders ripped out and footfalls pounded making Temple risk a glance over the top of the door.

The men who had been lying flat were hurrying into safety behind the buggy, while another man was running towards them. Luther made him pay for his brave move and a low shot to the side sent him spinning to the dirt. A second man had been moving to follow him out but he hurried back into cover.

'Stop admiring the view,' Hank said behind him, shoving the door along the ground for emphasis. 'And get moving.'

Temple took the strain on the door and they set off. The brief rest had helped them regain their strength and they managed a strong loping pace towards the horses. Another volley of shots tore through the door, but they were all through the edge of the wood where Temple had been before he'd moved back.

They reached the steps up on to the porch, where they faced the hardest task of coming out to secure the horses. Temple looked back at Hank for suggestions and saw that he was pointing at the base of the porch.

For most of its length the porch had short, white-painted rails, but on either side of the steps the rails had been fenced in. They lowered the door to the ground and went to their knees, allowing the door to lean against the posts on either side of the steps. Then they fast-crawled up the steps and rolled into hiding.

When Temple stopped he saw that Hank had gone the other way so that they were now flanking the steps. Temple gathered his breath, preparing to run for the horses from an unexpected position, but then he got a better result when the leader shouted out an order.

'Stop them getting in the house,' he called. 'It'll take forever to flush them out of there.'

Gunfire tore out, followed by a cry of pain showing that someone had tried to move out from the buggy and had then been dispatched by Luther. Then Emerson's men reverted to silence.

Long moments passed in which Temple lay

behind the solid planks on the porch, trying to work out what their attackers were doing. He wasn't able to raise himself enough to see the stables or the area around the buggy without risking being seen.

A decision must have been reached, for a thud sounded as the buggy was tipped over. Sustained gunfire tore out, but it was all directed at the door, which shook with every shot that holed it. Then the door slid down the posts to clatter to the ground on its back.

'The front door never opened,' someone shouted. 'They didn't go inside.'

'They're behind the fence,' the leader said.

Temple and Hank exchanged worried glances, acknowledging that their hidden spot wouldn't keep them safe for long. Then, worse, the horses bounded into view, kicking up their heels as they cantered away from the house.

'We waited for too long,' Hank said, shaking his head. 'We can't reach them now.'

'Then we do it later,' Temple said, moving himself up to a kneeling position. 'For now, we fight.'

Hank took a deep breath while he considered. He gave a brief nod, then knelt, adopting the same position as Temple had. Then, in a co-ordinated move, both men bobbed up, but they stilled their fire.

Their attackers were out of view, but a newcomer was riding through the gates. He was probably the only man who could stop this gunfight, even if he was the last man Temple had expected to see.

Emerson Merritt had arrived. He was swaying in the saddle, only his tight grip of the reins seemingly keeping him upright. His horse plodded to a halt beside the stables, where Emerson sat slumped in the saddle.

One of his men ventured out towards him while glancing around. When he looked to the house, Temple raised a hand, showing that he wouldn't be fired upon. The man hurried on to the horse to try to help Emerson down, although before he could lay a hand on him Emerson fell sideways and he had to catch him.

He helped him to stand and after a few moments Emerson gathered his strength and pushed his helper away. He stood bowed with his legs planted wide apart for balance, considering the scene.

'So the jailbreakers are here?' he demanded.

'We are,' Temple called, making Emerson shuffle round on the spot to look at him.

'Then you should have escaped while you still could.'

'We were trying to when your men tracked us down, not that I thought they'd be following your orders. The last I saw of you, you were bleeding to death.'

'I was found in time, no thanks to you.'

'I told Sheriff Simmons what had happened.'

'And he arrested you for killing me.' Emerson

snorted a laugh. 'I found him in the jailhouse. He's free now, but he's still clueless about where you've gone, as you'd expect of that worthless excuse for a lawman.'

While Emerson had been talking two men had come out from behind the buggy to drag the shot men away. Both the prone men stirred and groaned at their treatment.

'Then it's up to you what you tell him.' Temple pointed at the wounded men before they went out of view. 'We've got into an argument here, but those men are still alive. We can stop this turning into a bloodbath.'

'Why would I do that?'

'To let the truth about the Prairie Man come out.'

Emerson shook his head and walked slowly towards the buggy.

'He didn't attack me. I realize now that Miles Shaw drew my men away while Richard Cartwright stabbed me.' He spread his hands. 'The Prairie Man is irrelevant to all this, but you won't believe me. You're so convinced you're important, you can't see that what's happening has nothing to do with you, Hank, or the Prairie Man.'

Emerson reached the buggy and rested a hand on the corner to steady himself.

'So what is important?'

'Since James died a confrontation with the Rangers has been inevitable. The problem James

couldn't solve is what do you do when the law's inef-
fective. George Fowles's answer was to form his
group, but those of us with longer memories know
that's not the answer.'

Emerson glanced down at his men and made a
brief gesture. Temple didn't know what it meant, but
he caught glimpses of several men moving to new
positions.

'So your answer is to form your own group to keep
the peace, except they'll deliver your version of
justice.'

Emerson walked his hand along the buggy's side-
board so that he could turn to face Temple.

'You still don't understand that that's always the
problem with vigilante groups. The Prairie Man
knew that, and now you'll learn the hard way too.'

With Emerson revealing new information for the
first time, Temple started to shout out a demand for
him to explain what he meant, but Emerson had
already dropped out of view.

A moment later, as one, his men swung into view.
They slapped their guns on top of the buggy and
every one was aimed at them.

CHAPTER 13

Another volley of lead tore through the porch fence, repeatedly holing it.

Only the fact that Temple had thrown himself on to his chest saved him. On the other side of the steps Hank had also survived unscathed so far, but Temple wasn't sure for how much longer they could withstand the barrage.

Running for cover would be unlikely to work either, as wild gunfire was shattering the windows and splintering the door. Temple didn't know how Luther was faring in the stables, but he wasn't being effective.

When the gunfire ended Temple looked to Hank, hoping he might suggest an idea, but he looked at him with worried eyes. Then, in a reckless act, he jumped up and splattered gunfire back at the buggy. Temple joined him, but the men had stayed down.

The moment he and Hank dropped down to

reload they returned gunfire. This time they holed the porch badly and several broken planks that had at least been providing some protection toppled over, cutting down the area where he could lie.

The next time they fired they would know exactly where he was.

Temple looked around, weighing up his chances. He judged that the house provided his best option. He glanced at Hank who nodded. After a co-ordinated countdown they both leapt up and peppered gunfire over their shoulders at the buggy.

Hank took the window on his side of the door and Temple took the one on his. He ran across the porch, covering three paces while firing at every step before someone risked firing back.

That initial shot encouraged the rest to blast a deluge of lead at them. Temple abandoned firing. He put his head down, pounded the last pace, then threw his arms up and leapt through the window.

The panes had already been broken and he slammed through the few remaining pieces of glass, using his forearms to brush them aside. He turned his dive into a roll before he hit the floor on his back, then completed two rolls before he fetched up against a table.

He lay gathering his breath and flexing his limbs, finding that he'd completed his dash to cover without injury. He looked to the other window where Hank was lying on the floor, also grinning at his good fortune on reaching relative safety. Then both men edged to their respective windows to look out.

Men were seeking to reach either side of the house. Luther wasn't firing at them as he had problems of his own to worry about.

Two men had pressed their backs to the stable wall and they were out of his view from the loft. They were looking at each other co-ordinating the moment when they should slip inside.

Inside the house Temple and Hank both slammed their forearms on the sill of their respective windows for support. Then they took beads on the men running to the sides.

These men saw them and loosed off wild gunshots that clattered through the windows, shattering a few dangling shards of glass, but neither of their targets allowed themselves to be distracted.

Temple fired, then Hank. Temple's target went spinning into the end of the porch, where he held on to the rail for a moment before sliding down it. Hank's target staggered on for several paces before keeling over into the dirt.

They both waited for the next man to risk showing himself, but the other men stayed down behind the buggy. So Temple grunted a quick order to Hank to keep the buggy covered while he took aim at the men by the stables. These men were slipping in through the door, each man taking a separate side while peering up at the loft as they looked for Luther.

Temple gave them something else to worry about and fired three quick shots. They all struck high and before he could judge the distance better the men hurried inside and out of view. But his gunfire had worried them into being reckless and shots sounded within.

One man came staggering outside where he held on to the edge of the doorway before falling.

Silence reigned again. Then two rapid shots echoed, followed by a faint thud, possibly of a body hitting the ground. Temple waited, but nobody showed.

'I hope that wasn't Luther,' Hank said. 'He was a good man.'

'Yeah,' Temple said, avoiding giving any of the other replies that sprang to mind. Although he hadn't planned it that way, in the end Luther had sought his own redemption trail and he hoped it had given him peace.

A few moments later Temple saw that Luther's trail hadn't ended yet.

Luther peered out through the doorway and gave them a brief wave. Then he looked at the buggy, jerking his head from side to side as he sought a sighting of their assailants. He shook his head then looked at them and shrugged.

With Luther having dispatched two men as had

Temple and Hank, and with two men having been wounded earlier, they were now almost evenly matched. So perhaps Emerson's remaining men were being cautious, but as the minutes dragged on with nobody showing, it became increasingly likely that they were trying to draw them out.

'If this is a waiting game,' Hank said, 'we can't win it.'

Temple nodded. They were the ones who needed to get away and every moment that passed increased the probability that someone would come to investigate.

'Cover me,' Temple said. 'I'll make the first move.'

He checked that both sides were clear outside, then brushed away the debris from the window and swung over the sill to stand on the porch. With his back to the wall he looked for signs of where the remaining men had gone to ground while in the stable doorway Luther did the same.

They nodded to each other. Then they both started moving forward.

Temple slipped across the porch, then down the steps, aiming to move to a position side-on to the buggy, from where he could see behind it. Luther moved in the opposite direction, taking in the depression where some of the men had originally hidden themselves.

Temple couldn't shake off the feeling that they

were walking into a trap, but with time pressing they had no choice but to keep walking.

Slowly the other side of the buggy came into view, but nobody was there. He looked back to the house, then moved to the left to let the side become visible, again without luck.

He shot a glance at Luther, who turned on the spot, searching for their attackers. Then he too looked to the side of the house.

He flinched. His arm came up to point at the house a moment before a cry went up.

Temple saw movement beyond the window through which Hank had been looking and he realized what had happened. When they'd leapt through the windows the men had spread out and surrounded the house. Temple and Hank had dispatched the ones at the front but the others had slipped in through a back door.

Now Hank was tussling with someone.

Temple broke into a run. Luther sprinted over to join him, but Temple reached the porch a few paces ahead of him and put a shoulder to the door. He burst in, the door catching and making him stumble inside, but that unplanned motion saved him from a rapid burst of gunfire that sprayed into the door above his head.

Temple went to one knee and picked out the man who had fired, hitting him in the chest with a single shot. As the man toppled over, Temple checked the rest of the room, seeing only Hank and his assailant.

The man had trapped Hank against the wall and was seeking to push him down to the floor. Hank had been disarmed, but he had saved himself by wrapping an arm around his opponent's chest while holding his gun arm stretched out.

Temple didn't dare fire for fear of hitting Hank. Instead he hurried across the room.

He was two paces from them when Luther came bursting in through the window. The noise made the assailant look at him, this distraction heartening Hank into pushing him away.

The man walked backwards into Temple, who helped Hank by wrestling with him, but the man's brisk movement made him slip and all three men went tumbling to the floor in a huddle.

A gunshot roared as the pressure on the assailant's gun squeezed out a slug.

They all tensed before the man flopped to lie flat. Then Temple and Hank raised themselves to confirm that the man had managed to shoot himself. Temple looked at Hank and both men mustered smiles, but then from behind Luther coughed.

'It's over,' he said, his voice low and defeated.

Temple was facing the window. Slowly he turned to see that while they'd been tussling Emerson had led his remaining men into the room.

Three men were lined up with guns trained on them.

'You put up a good fight,' Emerson said. His expression was determined, but his eyes were tired. He moved over to sit at a table where he breathed deeply while considering them.

'As did you,' Temple said. 'So what happens now?'

'You die,' Emerson said with his eyes closed. The comment made the gunslingers firm their gun arms in anticipation of the order.

'As will you. The Rangers won't accept what you did here.'

'They'll find the bodies of three men who broke out of jail lying alongside the men they killed when they tried to escape. What George Fowles decides to do will be interesting and will show how committed to peace he is.'

Temple gestured at the two bodies in the room.

'This isn't any kind of peace that I know.'

'That is irrelevant.'

Emerson started to raise an arm, the movement slow and weak. The gunslingers were glaring at their three captives and didn't notice the movement.

Temple reckoned he heard a commotion going on outside. He wasn't sure what he'd heard, but it was likely that someone had found them. It could be Sheriff Simmons, but right now Temple would accept anyone intervening.

'Tell me why,' he said, speaking loudly to cover the sounds of brisk footfalls outside and to keep Emerson talking for a few more seconds.

141

Emerson converted the motion of making a signal into rubbing his brow before he looked at him, with his hand propping up his head.

'You want me to explain to you why you're irrelevant?'

'No. Before you have us shot tell me what this has all been about. Tell me about the Prairie Man.'

Despite the fraught situation Hank leaned forward in interest while Luther shot him an incredulous look. Then he glanced at the window, clearly having heard something too.

'Yeah,' Luther said, speaking loudly. 'I had nothing to do with any of this. If I'm to die because of some childhood story, I want to know why.'

'You're just playing for time,' Emerson muttered. 'It won't—'

Emerson's gaze darted to the window. His right eye twitched.

'Put those guns down,' George Fowles said, stepping into view through the window. 'You're surrounded.'

Emerson glared at him, but heavy footfalls sounded on the porch, confirming the rangers had been sneaking up on the house. Two rangers appeared at the other window, followed by more men moving into the doorway.

To a signal from George, three rangers rushed in through the door. One man went left, another went right, and the third knelt. With the room covered they took stock of the situation.

Seeing no option, Emerson signified that his gun-slingers should raise their hands. Only then did George come in to consider him.

'Before you arrived,' Emerson said, 'I was telling these men that I was looking forward to seeing you again.'

'Except you've lost,' George said.

'This isn't about winners and losers. It's about whose version of justice prevails. Now we'll find out if you're on the side of the lawmakers or the law-breakers.'

'The rangers keep the peace.'

'Even when some of the people breaking that peace are members of your own family?'

George turned to consider the three men. He nodded to Temple and smiled briefly at Hank.

'Even then,' he said. 'I'm sorry, Hank. I may have stopped Emerson shooting you up, but that doesn't mean I can accept you breaking the law. You three are going back to jail.'

CHAPTER 14

The main road was deserted when the four men stopped on the edge of town.

Half of the rangers had accompanied them while the other half watched over Emerson and his men as they dealt with clearing up the mayhem they'd caused. The ones who had come to town had stopped 200 yards back, leaving George Fowles to accompany Temple, Hank and Luther on the final leg.

George had claimed that this would give the appearance of them having returned of their own volition. He hoped this sign of repentance might sway Sheriff Simmons.

None of them believed that this was likely.

'I hope you can live with yourself,' Hank said, looking at the law office.

George sighed. 'I have no choice. I'll never be able to keep the peace if I operate to a different set of rules for family members.'

'Will that matter if you don't have a family any more?'

George lowered his head, accepting that he was risking a lot with this course of action.

'I know you won't forgive me for this, but I will speak up for you. Emerson's actions were odd. He knows something. When he's rested, I'll bring him to town and force him to tell Simmons what he knows. I will get to the truth, but I can't do that if you're free.'

Temple acknowledged the sense of this with a curt nod, but Hank could only shake his head.

'Then do it,' he said, moving his horse on, 'so you can get back to your precious rangers.'

Temple and George followed him, but Luther loitered, forcing George to beckon him on.

'As this is clearly a family affair,' Luther said, shaking his head. 'I don't need to bother the lawman. I'll be in the saloon.'

'You won't,' George said. 'Only the full story will help now, and you're a part of it.'

Luther grumbled, but he did move on to join them.

At the law office they dismounted. Hank said nothing more as he waited for someone else to take the lead. George was stern-faced showing that following his self-imposed rules was making him pay a heavy toll.

With a roll of the shoulders, Temple led the way to the door. As he entered the first person to see him was Kate. She was in consultation with her lawyer and they both looked at him with incredulous stares that grew even more astonished when Hank and the others followed him in.

'I thought I'd never see you again,' she murmured.

'You can thank—' Hank snapped before he bit back what he'd been planning to say. When he spoke again he used a softer tone. 'I couldn't run away from my troubles. I'm innocent and only guilty men run.'

'Men run for plenty of reasons,' Sheriff Simmons said, coming in from the jailhouse. 'And men stay put for plenty of reasons too.'

'I knew I wouldn't get fair treatment from you, but I came back anyhow. That must tell you something.'

'It does. The rangers caught you.' Simmons cast George an aggrieved glare, showing how hard it had been for him to make that declaration.

Everyone stood silently as an awkward silence dragged on until Simmons signified that Hank should return to the jailhouse first. Hank nodded forlornly to everyone, then moved to comply with the order, but Temple raised a hand.

'Wait,' he said. 'We need to discuss this.'

'There's nothing to discuss,' Simmons said. 'Judge Canby gave his directions and I'm not disobeying him.'

'Except he didn't know all the details, and I reckon neither does anyone else yet. Emerson and you and perhaps others know a part of a story, but nobody has pieced it all together. You need to do that. Then you need to get the judge back here.'

'Emerson won't be able to help.'

'Emerson told me that the Prairie Man knew about vigilante justice and that's tied in with why he and you hate the rangers. And Hank saw him, and that means he's the key to all this.'

Hank nodded. 'I saw him fifteen years ago and then again at James Merritt's house when I found his body.'

'You didn't,' Simmons muttered. He ushered Hank towards the jailhouse. 'And even if you did see someone recently, you wouldn't recognize him as being the same man.'

Temple stepped forward. 'I wasn't talking about Hank seeing the Prairie Man recently. I was interested in his sighting fifteen years ago. That's the important one.'

Simmons continued moving Hank on to the door, but after he'd opened it, he turned to Temple.

'Why?'

'Hank was only a kid, but what he saw that night is vital.' Temple looked at Hank.

Hank shrugged, but Temple's earnest gaze made him look aloft as he cast his mind back.

'It's hard to remember that far back,' he said. 'But

I saw a shape moving through the grass on the other side of the water, a man in a long coat, I suppose. He was moving quickly and I thought he was chasing me, so I ran.' Hank rocked his head from side to side. 'But he never came, so perhaps I was wrong.'

Temple waited, but Hank blew out his cheeks as he struggled to add more, so Simmons grabbed his arm and swung him into the jailhouse.

'Or perhaps,' Temple shouted after him, 'he didn't chase you because he was the one who was being chased.'

Simmons's footfalls stomped as he came to a halt. He stood for a moment, then poked his head back out through the doorway.

'Everyone but Temple will be gone when I return,' he said in a matter-of-fact manner. 'I will speak to him alone.'

As Simmons dealt with locking up Hank, everyone looked at the others, questioning what to do next. George broke the silence by going to Kate and ushering her to the door.

'Come on,' he said. 'We need to see what we can do to delay this while Temple does what he can.'

Kate cast Temple an imploring look before she and the lawyer followed him outside.

Luther loitered to wink at him. 'It looks as if I might have got away with this. So the best of luck.'

Temple returned the wink. Then, after Luther had hurried outside, he waited for Simmons to emerge.

Presently Simmons came back, sporting a pensive expression. He paced back and forth twice before he sat on the edge of his desk and considered him.

'There never was a Prairie Man,' he said.

'But Hank said he—'

Simmons raised a hand silencing him. 'I'll explain. Someone was lurking around outside the settlement. We chased him away, but he kept coming back and stealing. Then one day he went too far. We found your parents dead. We had no law to turn to so we decided to catch him ourselves.'

'So that's what Emerson meant about vigilantes?'

Simmons nodded. 'We caught him after a chase down by the creek. That's what Hank saw that night. But when we'd cornered him, we found that he was no man. He was just a lad, barely much older than you would have been back then. Our desire for summary justice took a battering, but some of the settlers were still determined to kill him, especially the ones who'd seen the bodies.'

'You killed him?'

'No. I stepped in and saved him. Redemption City was two weeks away, but I volunteered to take him there and let someone in authority decide what to do with him.'

'And what did they do?'

'Nothing. I let him go.'

Temple offered a smile. 'That doesn't sound like you.'

149

Simmons returned a brief smile. 'That was the last time I let personal feelings sway me. After ten days on the journey I accepted he was no killer. The lad had just been cold and hungry. Branding him as a killer stopped us from having to admit the truth. Your parents weren't nice people. You were better off living with Hank and Kate.'

Temple narrowed his eyes. 'Are you saying someone else killed them?'

Simmons shrugged. 'Possibly. It wasn't the kid. I'd guess your parents were arguing again and that they killed each other with their last dying breaths. I couldn't risk the kid suffering because of that, so I left him in the first town I came to.'

'And you never told anyone?'

'There were suspicions, but they weren't strong enough to stop people thinking I'd make a good lawman. And when the town grew I did become a lawman, but whether I made a good one is another question.'

'And now the Prairie Man is back, older and perhaps not as grateful as he should be?'

Simmons lowered his head and didn't reply for several seconds. When he did his voice was barely audible.

'Perhaps.'

Temple slammed a fist on the desk. 'I knew it. Hank is innocent and you're letting him go to the gallows because admitting the Prairie Man's returned will force you to reveal your mistake.'

'My mistake was to show compassion, the very thing you say I need to show now. Yet I'm doing now what I should have done then, my duty.'

'Then do it.' Temple turned to the door. 'I'll find the Prairie Man for you.'

'I've looked,' Simmons shouted after him. 'But I don't know who I'm looking for. He was just a kid the last time I saw him.'

The comment made Temple stop at the door. Lost for a reply, he glanced at the board that displayed Wanted posters. He turned, holding on to the door, a thought tapping at his mind.

'These posters,' he said, 'are they just for local crimes?'

'Mainly,' Simmons said, getting off his desk to walk towards him. His tone showed more interest as he noticed Temple's thoughtful expression. 'Are you thinking that if the Prairie Man is back, he's likely to have committed other crimes?'

'Yes.' Temple released the door to consider the posters more carefully. One was for a robbery at the station in Bear Creek. He tapped it. 'I passed through there on my way here. Some men robbed a mercantile and a kid got killed.'

Simmons shook his head. 'Not heard about that.'

'I met a man who said he was heading this way in search of the bounty on the robbers' heads. Apparently others were coming too.'

'I've not seen no bounty hunters.' Simmons snorted a harsh laugh. 'Perhaps you should leave the investigating to me.'

'Perhaps I should,' Temple said. He left the law office.

In a thoughtful mood he walked along the boardwalk to the nearest saloon. To his relief Luther was inside, propping up the bar. Luther glanced his way then beckoned him over.

'Simmons mention me?' he asked.

'Nope,' Temple said.

Luther breathed a sigh of relief, then took a glass and poured Temple a measure of whiskey.

'In that case I won't question my luck. I'll move on.'

'Before the bounty hunters catch up with you?'

'Sure.' Luther looked around the saloon as if these men might already be here. 'I assume you won't be coming with me now?'

'No. I'll keep my head down and hope they ride on by while they're chasing you.'

'Don't worry. I'll lead them a merry dance, and if Hank gets out of this mess, it'll make me feel that at least I've done some good.'

Temple nodded and took his whiskey. He sipped it, then smiled.

'You did, and I hope things go well for you.' He leaned on the bar beside him. 'Before this messy situation started, we enjoyed some good times together.'

'We didn't,' Luther said. He downed the last of his whiskey. 'We were only together for a day and that was a disaster.'

'Were we? I guess I must have been too drunk to remember everything.' Temple rubbed his brow. 'How did we meet up?'

Luther contemplated the empty glass before he placed it down on the bar.

'You were roaring drunk over a woman and if I hadn't have stepped in, you'd have been in the middle of a fearsome fight.'

Temple gave an uncertain nod, even though he remembered their meeting. He wanted to hear Luther's version.

'If you say so, but there must have been some- thing about me that interested you, as before long we were working together and up to no good.'

'Perhaps you looked just desperate enough to want to work for me.' Luther tipped his hat and walked around Temple to head to the door.

Temple swung round to follow his progress.

'But tell me,' he said, stopping him a few paces on, 'what exactly did I say and do that night that made you help me out?'

'Why?' Luther said, his tone becoming cautious as he turned.

'I don't want to go down that trail again. So what made me interesting? Was it my abilities? Was it my winning smile?' Temple smiled then hardened his expression. 'Or did I tell you about my life and how it'd gone wrong? Did I tell you that I came from Prudence?'

Luther narrowed his eyes. Taking that as a warning that he'd worked out where this conversation was going, Temple reached for his gun. Luther threw his hand to his holster, but before the gun could clear leather Temple had his six-shooter drawn and trained on his chest.

Luther stilled his motion with his gun half-drawn.

'Why have you gone and done that?' he said levelly.

'Because I've finally worked out who you really are.' Temple settled his stance. 'You're the Prairie Man.'

CHAPTER 15

'If you could figure that out,' Luther said, then snorted a laugh, 'you'll make a better lawman than Simmons ever could.'

'You covered your tracks well and Simmons only saw you as a kid,' Temple said, 'but what I don't understand is, he treated you well. Why do this?'

'He did, so I didn't come back to kill him and neither did I aim to harm you. I came for the others who wanted to kill me despite the fact I didn't do nothing wrong.'

Temple nodded, accepting Luther's word that he hadn't killed his parents.

'You still had a life you might not have had.'

'Not a good one. After Simmons left me, I ended up working for a merchant who beat me every day whether I worked hard or not. Then one day some men robbed him.' Luther smiled. 'One man put a hand over his mouth until he choked.'

'Just like the kid you claimed you killed in Bear Creek?'

Luther nodded. 'Except you've already worked out that that was a lie.'

'I assume that deception served its purpose when it made Burton run without his share of the money.' Temple watched Luther smile, confirming that this was the reason. 'And now?'

'And now I'll leave to kill Emerson. Whoever attacked him didn't know what they were doing. But then it'll end. He's the last of the ones who wanted to lynch me.'

'You know I can't let you do that.'

'You have no choice. If you kill me, nobody will believe that a childhood story came back.'

For long moments the two men stared at each other. Then Luther offered a placating smile, shrugged and turned to leave. But the motion had been designed to mask him drawing his gun.

He turned back, his gun swinging up, but he was too slow.

Temple knew Luther well enough to have anticipated the move. He fired, the gunshot hitting him low and making him double over.

With his free hand Luther clutched his stomach, then staggered sideways. He walked into the bar where he leaned on it with his face set in a pained grimace.

'But they will,' Temple said, 'because you're going

156

to explain it to them.'

Luther breathed deeply. He pushed away from the bar and forced himself to twist towards Temple. He uttered a roar of bravado as he jerked his gun towards Temple.

Twin gunshots blasted and for a terrible moment Temple thought that Luther had managed to fire too, but then Luther keeled over to reveal Sheriff Simmons standing in the doorway.

'Fifteen years too late,' Simmons said. 'But I did my duty in the end.'

'So you're not staying?' Temple said.

Hank looked out through his window at the swaying grass, as Temple had often done before he left.

'Too much has happened,' Hank said, 'for me to be happy here now.'

'I said that once, a long time ago.'

'And you returned,' Hank said, turning to him.

'I did.'

Temple joined him at the window.

Two days ago Hank had been freed after Judge Canby had accepted the new version of events with which Simmons had provided him. The lawman's fear that the news of his act of compassion fifteen years ago and how it had resulted in the spate of recent deaths would make people look at him differently had not yet been realized.

Even Emerson Merritt had accepted the news with grim solemnity, appearing relieved that the information about his role in the unfortunate incident was now known.

'Roaming clearly did you plenty of good,' Hank said. 'I hope it does the same for me.'

Temple frowned, not wishing to mention his many missed opportunities and mistakes, although in a way Hank had been right. In the end he'd worked out what was the right thing to do.

'I'll check in on Kate and her new child,' Temple said, 'and keep your home tidy. The rest of the time I'll keep the rangers in line.'

'Sheriff Simmons needs someone working with George whom he can trust. You'll do a fine job and that should stop the arguments about who can provide the best justice here.'

With those matters discussed there was nothing else that the two men needed to say to each other. They headed outside and paced down to the creek for one last time.

'You saved my life here.' Temple pointed at the water. 'No matter where you go, I'll never forget that.'

'And you saved my life here. No matter where I go, I'll never forget that.' Hank smiled. 'As you once said to me, if you ever need me, I will find you and I will save you.'

'I know.'

Hank moved for his horse, but he did so slowly and after dallying, he turned back.

They gave each other a quick pat on the shoulder, then on the back before they put aside their awkwardness and hugged briefly. Then Hank turned away quickly and went to mount his horse.

Standing on the top of the bank Temple watched Hank ride through the long grass down the side of the creek, then veer away.

For the next thirty minutes his form became smaller until he was just a distant speck. Long before he'd merged into the green of the prairies, Temple decided that from now on Hank would be the new Prairie Man.

When Kate had her family he would tell her children about the kindly shadow that had disappeared into the grass and how, if they were ever in trouble, they could always rely on one thing.

The Prairie Man would come and he would save them.